THE CLUE IN THE CRUMBLING WALL

When Nancy is asked to find a professional dancer who disappeared several years before, the young detective becomes involved in a mystery reaching far beyond a missing-person's case.

Clues lead to a huge estate which the dancer is to inherit if she can claim it in time. During Nancy's investigation at Heath Castle, she and her friends Bess Marvin and George Fayne realize that its crumbling walls contain a secret, but what is it? And who are their enemies that try to foil their every attempt to unravel the intricate puzzle?

Danger lurks in a castle tower and throughout the vine-tangled grounds of the estate. The girls' gripping adventures culminate in a dramatic climax when Nancy exposes a sinister plot to defraud the dancer of her inheritance.

"We must get out of here!" said Nancy.

NANCY DREW MYSTERY STORIES®

The Clue in the Crumbling Wall

BY CAROLYN KEENE

GROSSET & DUNLAP
Publishers • New York
A member of The Putnam & Grosset Group

Acknowledgement is made to Mildred Wirt Benson, who under the pen name
Carolyn Keene, wrote the original NANCY DREW books

Library of Congress Catalog Card Number: 73-2182 ISBN 978-0-448-09522-6
9 10 8

Contents

An Urgent Request

"HURRY, Nancy!" Hannah Gruen called anxiously. The Drews' housekeeper held the front door open as jagged lightning cut the sky.

Nancy raced madly toward the door, her reddish-blond hair flying in the wind. "Made it!" she gasped, laughing, as great drops of rain pelted the driveway.

The attractive, eighteen-year-old girl stepped into the hall and stopped in surprise. Behind Hannah stood a slender young policewoman in a blue uniform.

"This is Lieutenant Masters, dear," said Hannah. "She arrived just before your car turned into the driveway."

"I can't stay long, Nancy," the officer said, "so I'll come right to the point. Will you help solve a mystery?" The woman's dark eyes gazed into Nancy's steadily. "I'm sure you can do it."

Nancy was amazed, but merely said, "I'd like to hear about it. Won't you come in and sit down?" She led the officer into the living room.

Nancy's zest for adventure came to her naturally from her father, Carson Drew, a well-known lawyer. While helping him, she had solved her first case, *The Secret of the Old Clock*. Since then she had been successful in finding the solutions to several mysteries, the most recent one *The Secret in the Old Attic*. By now Nancy had an outstanding reputation, even with the police, as an amateur sleuth.

"Chief McGinnis recommended that I ask you," Lieutenant Masters said, seating herself on the sofa. "He told me you have great insight into character." The trim, dark-haired officer explained that she had just joined the River Heights Police Department. "This case is related to one of mine. I'm in charge of juvenile offenders."

"Then your mystery involves a child?"

"Yes. A pretty little eight-year-old girl named Joan Fenimore. She's been in trouble with the law and will be in more, I'm afraid, unless we can find her aunt. Nancy, have you ever heard of Juliana Johnson?"

"She was a dancer, wasn't she?" Nancy asked.

"Yes. She disappeared ten years ago at the height of her career."

"And she's Joan's aunt?"

"Yes. Juliana must be found within the next

three weeks or lose an inheritance that a friend willed to her. If we can find her, surely she'll help Joan and her mother and make a new way of life for Joan."

"Three weeks!" Nancy repeated. "That means I haven't a moment to lose!"

The lieutenant's grave face broke into a smile. "Then you'll take the case?" she said. "I'm so glad!" She glanced at her watch and rose quickly. "I must go now. The rain has stopped. I was on a call in this neighborhood and decided to drop by on the chance you were at home. Could you meet me at headquarters about three o'clock this afternoon?"

"Certainly," Nancy replied.

"Fine! I'll tell you all about it then, and we'll go see Joan and her mother. By the way," she added when they reached the door, "do you know Heath Castle, a big estate some miles outside of town?"

"Yes, I do," Nancy said. "I've seen it from the river. It's that spooky-looking place with those stone towers and the high walls around it."

"Find out all you can about the place," Lieutenant Masters said. "It's Juliana's inheritance. And thank you, Nancy. Little Joan really needs your help!"

After the policewoman had left, Nancy went to the kitchen and told Hannah about the mystery.

"Now you're happy!" the kindly, middle-aged woman said fondly. "You have a new case! I just hope it won't be dangerous." Mrs. Gruen had been with the family since the death of Mrs. Drew when Nancy was three years old. The warm-hearted housekeeper had always been like a mother to the girl.

"What do you know about Heath Castle?" Nancy asked her.

"Not much. It was built—"

"Hannah!" Nancy exclaimed. She was facing the window. "Look—in the yard!"

"What is it?" the housekeeper asked, peering through the glass. "Oh, what a shame!" she cried out. "All the hollyhocks are snapped off in the middle and the daisies are flattened into the mud from the rain!"

"That's not what I mean," said Nancy. "Look at the flower border where my new rosebushes were."

"Why, they're gone!" said Hannah. She stared in amazement at two holes filled with rain water.

"The bushes were dug up," said Nancy, "and stolen!"

"Probably by the same thief who took plants from some of our neighbors," Hannah remarked. "There's been a rash of these thefts lately."

"I'll report it when I go to headquarters this afternoon," Nancy said.

While she set the table and heated soup, Hannah made sandwiches. By the time the two had finished their lunch, the ground had dried a little and the sun was out.

They hurried into the back yard to inspect the damage. Except for the rosebushes, no plants were missing. Nancy could not find any clues to the thief. She and Hannah began cleaning up debris from the storm. Suddenly they heard the familiar song of one of River Heights' well-known eccentric characters.

"Here comes my old friend Salty down the street!" Nancy laughed, shaking off her somber mood.

The good-natured, elderly man, once a sailor, had received his nickname from Nancy when she was a little girl. He had introduced himself to the Drew household as Boatswain Bostwick Bumpleton, "home from the salty seas."

Nancy had tried to say his whole name but sometimes mixed it up. Once she addressed him as Bumple Boat and another time as Humpty Dumpty Bumpleton, much to his amusement. Finally the little girl settled on Salty and her nickname stuck to him.

The man's cart bell tinkled merrily, and a moment later the jolly, weather-beaten sailor wheeled his wagon around the corner of the driveway. Spying Nancy and Hannah, he sang again:

> "Clams by the bushel,
> Clams by the lot,

Clams for the kettle,
Clams for the pot."

"None for us today," Mrs. Gruen called.

Salty smiled. "Come now," he coaxed. "Ye can't turn down my clams. They're nutritious, delicious, delectable, respectable! Matter of fact, ye might even find a pearl in one of 'em!"

Nancy turned to Hannah. "Don't you think we could use a few pearly clams?" she asked with a wink.

The housekeeper gave in. "Okay, a dozen. Nancy, please get my purse."

Nancy darted away, but soon returned with the pocketbook and a container for the clams. After the elderly sailor had left, she and Hannah took the clams into the kitchen and Nancy started to open them with a sharp knife. Soon she had a pile of empty shells, but no pearls.

"I guess these haven't anything in them but meat! Well, here's the last one."

Nancy opened the clam and was about to toss away the attractive, rainbow-colored shell when a tiny object inside drew her attention.

"A pearl!" she cried, holding it out for the housekeeper to see.

Hannah stared at the small white object. "I declare, it *is* one," she acknowledged, "and may be worth some money!"

"I'll take it to Sam Weatherby," Nancy said eagerly. She removed the pearl and washed it,

"Ye might find a pearl in one of 'em!" Salty said.

then drove to Mr. Weatherby's shop. The owner was a dealer in curios and antique jewelry.

Nancy had to wait fifteen minutes while an unpleasant man bargained with the shop owner over a piece of jewelry he wanted to sell. It was a man's antique watch chain with an attractive gold charm. At last the customer accepted an offer, pocketed the money Mr. Weatherby paid him, and turned on his heel, remarking, "I might as well have given it to you!"

After the man had left, Mr. Weatherby said to Nancy, "That was Daniel Hector. How he loves to argue! If all my customers were like him, I'd have to close up shop. Well, what can I do for you, Nancy?"

She removed the pearl from her purse and asked the curio dealer what it was worth.

"Well, well," he said, examining the object carefully, "it's nice, but river pearls are not valuable." He named a modest sum. "I'll buy it if you'll bring me the shell from which it was taken. I want to display the pearl with the shell."

Nancy promised to return with the shell the next day. Then she put the pearl in her pocketbook and left the shop. She started walking the few crowded blocks to police headquarters.

As Nancy stopped to look in the window of a department store, a boy drew close to her. Then suddenly he jerked the purse from beneath her arm and fled!

CHAPTER II

Heath Castle

IT took Nancy a moment to recover from her astonishment. By the time she whirled around, the purse snatcher was already running down the street. Nancy dashed after him, but tried to avoid bumping into pedestrians.

"What's the matter?" asked a man she side-stepped just in time to avoid a collision.

"My purse—"

He took up the chase with her. As word spread, other people followed. But the boy was running fast. Nancy caught a glimpse of him as he dashed into a narrow alley between two buildings. When she reached it, there was no sign of him.

"Well, there goes my pearl," she thought unhappily.

Besides the pearl, her purse had contained her driver's license, car registration, some credit cards, money, and cosmetics.

"I suppose I should be thankful I didn't lose more," Nancy said to herself ruefully.

She thanked the stranger who had tried to assist her, then hurried down the street to headquarters and was taken into Lieutenant Masters' office.

After greetings were exchanged, Nancy said, "I want to report two thefts." First she told about the boy who had snatched her purse.

"Can you describe him?" the policewoman asked.

"I didn't get a look at his face," said Nancy, "but I think he was about ten or twelve years old. He was stocky with tousled blond hair and wore blue jeans and a tee shirt."

"Many boys could fit that description," Lieutenant Masters commented. "We'll do our best, but I doubt that you'll get back your bag with the contents." Then she frowned. "Did I hear you say 'two thefts'?"

"Yes," said Nancy, and told about the missing rosebushes.

The officer's dark eyes gleamed with interest. "I think I can give you the answer to the second one right away," she said. "The culprit is probably little Joan Fenimore."

"Oh no!" Nancy said in dismay.

"Yes," said the officer. "I told you she had been in difficulty with the law. Just before I came to see you I was checking into another report of flowers stolen from your neighborhood. The woman of the house caught a glimpse of the child and described her.

"Joan has a passionate love for flowers," Lieutenant Masters went on, "and an amazing knowledge of them. I arranged for her to join a nature study class at the museum, but I'm afraid that my rehabilitation program backfired. Recently she has taken plants and shrubs from other homes."

"What a shame!" Nancy said.

"Joan's father is not living," the young officer resumed. "Her widowed mother is ill and very poor."

Nancy listened sympathetically as the policewoman went on, "I'll see that Joan returns the bushes to your garden. Mrs. Fenimore will insist upon it, anyway. She's greatly distressed by her child's behavior."

Lieutenant Masters stood up. "Come along," she said. "We'll go there now and you can hear everything firsthand."

The two rode to the Fenimore house located in a run-down section of the city. The tiny yard was a mass of colorful flowers, however, and vines half-covered the unpainted, weather-beaten porch.

As Nancy and the officer went up the flagstone walk, the policewoman called attention to two young, newly planted rosebushes.

"Are these yours?" she asked.

"They look like the ones that were in our yard," Nancy said. "But—"

She broke off, because a little girl in a faded pink dress had just come around the corner of the house. When the child saw the woman in uniform, she stopped short and then turned as if to run off.

"Don't be afraid," the lieutenant said gently.

"Did you come to take me away?" Joan asked.

"Indeed we didn't. But we will have to send you to a special school unless you decide to be good."

"I am good," Joan said, tossing her tangled blond curls. "Just ask my mother!"

"In many ways you are very good. I know you work hard to take care of your mother. But why do you dig up shrubs and plants that don't belong to you?"

Joan's gaze roved to the telltale rosebushes. She hung her head and didn't answer.

"I'm sure you don't really mean to be naughty," the policewoman continued. "Why do you take flowers?"

"Because they're pretty," Joan said. "We can never buy anything nice."

The child sank down on the porch steps and began to cry. Lieutenant Masters comforted her. Soon she gained an admission from the little girl that an older boy, Teddy Hooper, who lived next door, had suggested that Joan help herself to some pretty plants.

"I don't know why I did it." Joan began to sob. "I wish my Aunt Juliana would come home. I'm sure she'd buy us some nice things."

In an undertone Lieutenant Masters explained to Nancy that Joan knew about her aunt only from her mother.

"Mrs. Fenimore wasn't married when her sister disappeared. Come inside and let her tell you the story."

Nancy received a distinct shock as Joan led the way into the living room. Lying on a well-worn couch was a slender woman with deep lines in her pallid face. Nancy was sure Mrs. Fenimore was not more than thirty years old, but she looked fifty.

Upon seeing the policewoman, a concerned expression appeared on Mrs. Fenimore's face. "Has Joan done something wrong again?"

At her mother's question, the child turned her head away. Neither Lieutenant Masters nor Nancy spoke immediately. After a brief pause, the police officer introduced the new visitor.

"I'm glad to meet you," Mrs. Fenimore said softly.

"I'm sorry you're not feeling well," Nancy replied. "Perhaps it would be better if I came back some other time."

"No, no."

"I wish you'd tell Nancy Drew about your sister," Lieutenant Masters urged. "Nancy's a detective and will try to find out what happened to Juliana."

"You really will?" Mrs. Fenimore looked at the girl hopefully. "You see, Julie went away by herself for a month's rest and never was heard of again."

"Have you any idea at all where she may have gone?" Nancy asked. "Do you think she disappeared deliberately?"

"No. I can't believe that, and I keep telling Joan I'm sure her aunt will come home someday."

Mrs. Fenimore explained that the dancer had been engaged to a wealthy manufacturer named Walter Heath.

"Five years after her mysterious disappearance, he died and left Heath Castle to Juliana. He tried to trace her before his death but was unsuccessful. There's a provision in his will which stipulates that if Juliana does not claim his estate within five years, it is to be sold and the money given to charities he specified. The time is almost up."

After a pause Mrs. Fenimore went on, "The grounds of Heath Castle were beautiful once, with walled gardens and sunken pools. Now I'm told it looks like an overgrown jungle, full of weeds. Nevertheless, I am hoping Julie will be found and can come to claim the castle."

The story deeply interested Nancy. She could hardly wait to begin the search for the missing dancer. She was also eager to visit Heath Castle! She mentioned this to Mrs. Fenimore.

The woman smiled. "I'll lend you a key to the front door that Walter left with me to give to Julie. Joan dear, bring my jewel case here."

The little girl hurried off to get it. In a few moments she returned with the box. Her mother took the key from inside and handed it to Nancy. "I wish you luck," Mrs. Fenimore said.

Before Nancy and Lieutenant Masters left the house, they helped Joan prepare supper for herself and her mother. Wishing to spare Mrs. Fenimore any further worry, they refrained from discussing the child's thieving instincts in depth.

As they drove away, Nancy remarked, "It's possible Juliana met with foul play."

"Yes," said Lieutenant Masters. "If that's true, you may find yourself up against a dangerous adversary."

When the two young women walked into headquarters a little later, the desk sergeant said, "You're in luck, Miss Drew!" He held up her stolen purse. "A patrolman found it in a trash can. Nothing but the money and the pearl was taken."

Nancy was thrilled. "I'm especially glad to have my driver's license and car registration back," she said, "and the credit cards. Please thank the patrolman for me."

The following day Nancy related Mrs. Fenimore's story to her closest friends, Bess Marvin and George Fayne, who had dropped in. The two girls were cousins and helped Nancy when she was working on a mystery. Bess was blond and slightly plump. She was less inclined toward adventure than her spunky cousin, an attractive brunette, who liked athletics and was proud of having a boy's name.

Bess said soberly, "It's a shame about Joan and Teddy. I'll help you all I can with them."

George was eager to pursue work on the mystery. "What are we waiting for?" she asked. "Why not go now and explore the castle?"

Cautiously Bess asked, "Will it be safe?"

"It won't be easy," Nancy warned her friends. "I was told the undergrowth is like a jungle. Maybe the best way to get there is by motorboat up the Muskoka River."

Twenty minutes later the three girls rented a small motorboat at Campbell's Landing. The craft was old and the engine clattered and threw oil, but it was the only boat available.

"Lucky we all know how to swim," Bess said with some misgiving as they pulled away from the dock. "I have a feeling this old tub leaks and may sink before we go very far."

"We'll be all right if George keeps busy with the bailer!" Nancy laughed, heading the craft upstream.

The river was wide near town, but the upper

reaches were narrow and twisted and turned at such sharp angles that fast travel was out of the question. At the wheel, Nancy kept an alert watch for shoals. Water was slowly seeping in at the bow.

"It's really pretty out here, but so wild," Bess commented, her gaze wandering along the solid line of trees fringing the shores.

"Better forget the scenery for a while," Nancy advised, "and give George a hand with the bailing. If you don't, our shoes will be soaked."

The water was coming in faster now. Both Bess and George worked vigorously, dipping the water and throwing it over the side.

"Listen!" Nancy said presently. "What's that?"

Bess and George stopped bailing to look around. They had heard no unusual sound.

"Another boat!" Nancy exclaimed as the noise of an engine grew louder. "But where is it?"

Just then a small blue-and-white craft shot into view from Harper's Inlet, one of the river's many small hidden bays.

"Look out!" Bess cried in alarm.

The pilot in the oncoming boat seemed to be unaware of the girls in their little craft. At high speed he raced straight toward it. Desperately Nancy spun the wheel. There was not enough space to clear.

With a splintering crash the two boats collided!

CHAPTER III

A Runaway Boat

THE speeding boat which had struck the girls' craft now veered sharply away and raced downstream.

Meanwhile, the impact had caused Bess to lose her balance. She hit her head on the side of the boat and toppled into the water.

Instantly Nancy turned off the motor. If Bess were unconscious, there was no time to lose!

George had already dived over the side. When she located her cousin, she grasped the inert form with her left arm and struck out with the other for the boat. Nancy leaned over and helped pull the unconscious Bess aboard.

"Is she—?" Nancy began.

At that moment Bess opened her eyes and coughed several times. Nancy patted her on the back.

"I'm—all—right," Bess said weakly. "Our boat—" She tried to point.

For the first time the others realized that water was filling the craft at an alarming rate through a small hole in its side.

"Quick, George! Bail!" Nancy cried.

George picked up the bucket she had been using before and started to work. Nancy crumpled up a newspaper lying on the bottom of the boat and stuffed the hole with it. In a tackle box she found a small burlap sack, which she rolled up and added to the paper. In a moment the inflow of rushing water was reduced to a trickle.

"Good!" George panted and sat down. "Now we can chase that other boat!"

It was not in sight, however, and Nancy decided it would be useless to try pursuing the faster craft. She turned her attention to Bess.

"How are you feeling?" she asked.

"All right. But I'd like to go home."

"We will," said Nancy. "I'm afraid this boat can't stand much more."

"I wish we hadn't lost the fellow who ruined it," said George. "If I ever see him—"

"Would you recognize him?" Nancy asked.

George said she would not, and Bess had not gotten a good look at him either.

"I saw him," Nancy said slowly. "I'm sure I'd recognize his face. And he was thin and wore a light-blue cap."

The girls dreaded returning to Campbell's Landing with their damaged craft. But when the owner saw the damaged craft, he was not angry.

"It won't cost more than twenty-five dollars to repair it," he assured them. "My boat rental insurance will take care of it."

After saying good-by, Nancy drove her friends home. As Bess got out of the car, she said, "I'm sorry our trip to Heath Castle was ruined."

Nancy smiled. "We'll go another time."

The following day's investigation unearthed no clue to the identity of the boatman. Though Nancy described him and his blue-and-white craft to several persons, not one of them was able to identify it. Finally she thought of Salty the clam digger.

"I'll drive down to his place on the river and talk with him," she told Hannah Gruen. "He might also know something about the Heath estate."

Nancy invited Bess to go along and proceeded toward the river. Salty's home was very quaint. Once it had been a small, attractive yacht. Now it was a beached wreck, weathered by sun and rain. Its only claim to any former glory was the flag which flew proudly from the afterdeck.

"Anyone here?" Nancy called.

"Come in, come in!" the former sailor invited. He was sitting with his feet up on a built-in table and eating beans out of a can.

When he saw the girls, he stood up. "Ye honor me, comin' here," he said, his blue eyes twinkling. "But I'm goin' to have to disappoint ye. I've nary a clam today."

"Oh, we didn't come to buy clams," Nancy replied, glancing curiously at the furnishings of the yacht. The room was small and cluttered, but very clean. Salty's bunk was neatly made. On a shelf above it was an amazing array of sea shells.

"I collect 'em," the sailor explained, following Nancy's gaze. "Some o' those shells came from the Orient, an' some from right here in the Muskoka."

He walked over to the shelf and pointed to a curious specimen. "That's called the washboard clam. It's one o' the biggest of our river clams. And this is a whelk from the seashore. You can get dye out of it when the critter's fresh."

"How interesting!" the girls exclaimed.

Pleased by their attention, the man showed them other shells which were too large to stand on the narrow shelf. One, measuring three feet across, had come from an island in the Pacific.

Nancy grinned. "What a pearl that might hold!" She told of her own loss, saying she was glad the pearl was not large and valuable.

The former sailor showed the girls other treasures from the sea; huge fluted specimens and tiny, delicate shells. Amazed at the variety, Nancy asked Salty if he had collected them during his travels.

"No." The clam digger laughed. "Mr. Heath gave 'em to me."

The name startled Nancy. "Not Walter Heath?"

"No. Ira Heath—Walt's father," Salty answered. "He gave me the shells when he had his button factory on the inlet."

"A button factory near here?" Bess asked in surprise.

"It's been closed for years. It was shut down when the supply o' fresh-water mussels gave out. Mollusk mother-of-pearl shells are used, you know, to make pearl buttons."

"What became of Mr. Heath?" Nancy inquired.

"Ira was born in England an' went back there on a visit. He died in London. His son Walt was left in charge here."

"Did Ira build the castle?" Bess asked.

Salty nodded, warming to the story. "Yes, Heath Castle was built to look like one o' those fancy English places. The gardens were beautiful—a sight to set your eyes ablaze with admiration. Stone walls everywhere, with flowers an' vines, an' all kinds o' trees from everywhere in the world."

Nancy was becoming more eager every minute to see the estate.

"But for me," Salty went on, "the place is too

lonesome. No houses close by. The old gent built it 'bout a mile up the river from the button factory. Walter lived in it, too, an' he used to do some o' his scientific experimentin' there."

"What kind of experiments?" Nancy asked.

"Don't know," said Salty. "Since Walt died, no one ever goes near the castle, or the factory on Harper's Inlet."

"Harper's Inlet?" Nancy repeated thoughtfully. "Someone must have been there yesterday."

"That's right," Bess agreed. "We saw a motorboat coming out of the inlet. It crashed into our boat."

"Queer," Salty commented. "I don't know what business anyone would have at the factory. Who was the fellow?"

"That's what we came to ask you," Nancy replied.

She gave a complete account of the incident. Salty could not identify the man or his boat from her description, but he promised to watch for such a person.

"I'll keep an eye out for the boat, too," he added. "Can't figure what the fellow would be doin' there. Fishin's no good there. Maybe I'll run up an' have a look."

Satisfied that Salty would be able to locate the boat if anyone could, Nancy and Bess thanked him and left.

As they stepped onto the dock they saw that the weather had changed. Dark clouds filled the sky and the wind was whipping the river into whitecaps.

"I wanted to visit Heath Castle today," Nancy said, "but it wouldn't be wise to take a boat out now."

"Let's do it tomorrow," Bess suggested.

"Then George can go with us," Nancy said.

A surprise awaited Nancy when she reached home. While she and Mrs. Gruen had been away, the two rosebushes had been replanted in the garden. They were only slightly wilted from having been moved twice.

"Oh, I'm so glad Joan brought them back!" Nancy declared. "I'm sure she wouldn't have taken them if that Hooper boy hadn't urged her to."

Nancy was pressing earth. firmly about the bushes when her father drove into the garage. She stopped her work and ran to greet him. Mr. Drew was a distinguished-looking man, tall and handsome.

"I'm happy you're back from your trip," she said.

"Hello, Nancy." He smiled. "How's the garden?"

"Better today. The rosebushes that were taken day before yesterday are home again."

The Drews went into the house together and

Nancy told him about the boat, the Fenimore problems, and the mystery of Juliana's disappearance.

"Dad, tell me all you can about Ira Heath and his son Walter," she said. "Did you know them?"

"Only by reputation. For years they operated a very successful pearl button factory. Then the business went to pieces."

"I already know that part," Nancy said. "What about Heath Castle? After Walter Heath died, who took charge of the place?"

"Daniel Hector is the executor, I believe."

Nancy's mind flew to the unpleasant customer in the curio dealer's shop.

"The lawyer?" she asked.

"Yes," Mr. Drew replied. "But I must say his sharp practice of law never appealed to me."

"Do you think Mr. Hector did everything possible to find Juliana?" Nancy asked thoughtfully.

"I believe so."

"Did you know her?"

"I saw her perform many times, and admired her dancing very much," Mr. Drew replied. "Why she disappeared at the height of her career has always puzzled me."

"Apparently she left no clues behind."

"The case was a strange one," her father said. "I guess her fiancé was pretty broken up over her disappearance. I've always wondered if he might have had something to do with it." After a pause he added, "Heath Castle might provide a key to the mystery."

"I was thinking the same thing!" Nancy exclaimed with a mysterious twinkle in her eyes. "Tomorrow I'll go there and take a look around that castle and those old walls!"

CHAPTER IV

The Haunted Walk

SHORTLY after breakfast the following morning, Nancy, Bess, and George drove to Heath Castle. By studying a map of the area, they had discovered a little-used road which led to the abandoned estate. Though this woodland route was rough and dusty, Bess preferred it to another boat trip.

"Hope we don't get a flat tire," Nancy remarked, maneuvering the car to avoid jagged rocks. "How much farther is it?"

George peered at the odometer and noted that they had traveled about five miles from the outskirts of River Heights.

"We're coming to something!" she exclaimed a moment later.

Through the trees the girls caught a fleeting glimpse of a tall tower. The car rounded a sharp curve, blotting it from view. Then the road ended abruptly in front of a high, vine-covered stone wall.

"The front boundary of the estate!" Bess announced. "There's the name Heath Castle on the gate."

Nancy jumped from the car and led the girls to the iron gate. It was fastened by a heavy iron chain, secured by a huge padlock.

"The key I have won't open this padlock," Nancy said. "It's for the front door."

"Who put the padlock on?" Bess asked.

"Probably Daniel Hector, the executor," George replied.

"Whoever it was is determined to keep everyone out," Nancy said thoughtfully.

"How do we get in?" Bess asked.

"Over the top, commando style," George urged. "Lucky we wore jeans."

Nancy and Bess looked with misgivings at the sharp iron spikes of the high, rusty gate.

"I don't like the idea of climbing over that. There must be an easier way to get in," Nancy said, her gaze roving along the crumbling, ivy-covered wall.

The girls walked alongside for some distance. Finally they came to a spot which was a bit lower than the gate and offered good toe holds. It was not difficult for them to grasp vines and pull themselves to the top. Bess was reluctant to go, but decided to follow. The three friends leaped down on the other side of the wall and started through the dense growth of trees and shrubs.

It was damp and cool beneath the canopy of leaves. There were many eerie noises. As they progressed, Bess said she felt very uneasy.

"Listen!" she commanded tensely. "What's that?"

"The cooing of a pigeon," Nancy replied. "Come along, or we'll all have the jitters."

Just ahead stretched a long avenue of oak trees, which the girls thought might lead to the castle. They tramped through the waist-high grass and came to a vine-tangled, fern-matted bower. Two handsome stone vases lay on their sides, broken. Apparently rain water had filled them and frozen during the winter, bursting the vases.

"What a shame this place is being neglected!" Nancy commented, pausing a moment. "Mr. Hector ought to take care of it. Surely there must be money in Mr. Heath's estate set aside for that purpose! If Juliana should come back, she would hardly recognize the place."

At the end of the oak-lined avenue, the girls came to a weather-stained loggia of stone. Its four handsomely carved pillars rose to support a balcony over which vines trailed. Steps led to the upper part.

After mounting to the balcony, Nancy and her friends obtained a fine view of the nearby gardens. They had been laid out in formal sections, each one bounded by a stone wall or an untrimmed hedge. Here and there were small circular pools, now heavy with lichens and moss, and fountains with leaf-filled basins. Over the treetops, about half a mile away, the girls could see two stone towers.

"That's the castle," said George.

Amid the wild growth, Nancy spotted a bridge. "Let's go that way," she suggested, starting down from the balcony.

In a few minutes the trio had crossed the rickety wooden span. Before them lay a slippery moss-grown path.

"The Haunted Walk," Nancy read aloud the name on a rustic sign.

"Why not try another approach?" Bess said with a shiver. "This garden looks spooky enough without deliberately inviting a meeting with ghosts!"

"Oh, come on!" Nancy laughed, taking her friend firmly by the arm. "It's only a name. Besides, the walk may lead to something interesting."

Spreading lilac bushes canopied the trail. Their branches caught at Nancy's hair and clutched at her clothing. Impatiently she pushed them aside and held back the branches for her friends to pass beneath.

"I wish we'd gone some other way," Bess complained. "This is no fun."

"I think it is," Nancy replied. "It's mysterious here! It's so—"

Her voice trailed away suddenly. George and Bess glanced at her quickly. Nancy was staring directly toward a giant evergreen.

"What is it?" Bess demanded fearfully.

"Nothing."

"You didn't act as if it were nothing," George said to Nancy.

"I thought I saw something, but I must have been mistaken."

Despite their coaxing, Nancy would not reveal what had startled her. For an instant she thought a pair of penetrating, human eyes had been staring at the girls from behind the evergreen. Then they had blinked shut and vanished.

"It must have been my imagination," Nancy told herself.

She walked on hurriedly. As Bess and George sensed her thoughts, they drew closer to the young detective. Nancy rounded the evergreen and saw that it partially hid a vine-covered, decaying summerhouse.

The building was empty, but her eye quickly caught a slight quivering of the vines beside the doorway, although there was no wind. She stopped short, struck by the realization that someone *had* been lurking there! Quietly she told the others.

"I knew we shouldn't have chosen this walk," Bess muttered. "It *is* haunted."

"Haunted by a human being," Nancy said grimly. "I wish I knew who was spying on us!"

There was no sign of anyone now. The girls heard neither the rustle of leaves nor the sound of retreating footsteps.

"Let's go back to the car," Bess proposed suddenly. "We've seen enough of this place."

"I haven't," Nancy said. "I'm getting more curious every minute."

Not far from the summerhouse was a stone wall. It occurred to Nancy that the person who had observed them might have scrambled over it to avoid detection. She announced her intention of climbing up to make sure.

While Bess and George watched uneasily, Nancy began to scale the vine-covered wall. Near the top, however, she lost her footing. With a suppressed cry, she fell backward!

George and Bess helped Nancy to her feet. Although uninjured, she was visibly shaken.

"I guess I'd better not try that again," she said ruefully.

"Those are the most sensible words I've heard you say today!" Bess declared. "Let's get out of here before we find ourselves in real trouble."

"I'm with you," George said. "I have an appointment in town, and anyway, it may rain."

Nancy was reluctant to leave the estate without exploring the castle, but she had noticed that clouds were darkening the sky.

"All right," she agreed. "But we'll come back!"

The girls retraced their way across the bridge. From that point on, however, they could not find the right direction to the road.

"We're probably a long way from the car," George said finally. "I'll climb a tree and see if I can spot it."

Nimble as a monkey, she went high among the branches. Then she shouted down that the river was close by and the road far away.

"We've wandered a great distance from where we started," George reported as she slid down the tree and pointed out the route. "We must cut straight through that woods ahead."

"Are you sure we won't get hopelessly lost?" Bess asked.

"Just follow me."

Nancy and Bess were quite willing to have George lead the way. She pushed ahead confidently, tramping down the high grass and thrusting aside thorny bushes. But as the going became more difficult, her pace slackened.

"It seems to me we're moving in a wide circle," Nancy said at last.

George paused to catch her breath. Her gloomy silence confirmed Nancy's suspicion.

"George, are we lost?" she asked.

"I don't know about you," the girl answered ruefully. "Myself—yes."

"It's going to rain any minute, too," Bess said,

sinking down on a mossy log. "Oh, why did we come to this horrible, gloomy place? Imagine anyone building a home here!"

"If the roads were opened and some shrubs cut down, the estate would be very lovely," Nancy pointed out.

After resting for a few minutes the girls decided to continue their trek. Nancy proved a better pathfinder than George and before long they came to recently trampled grass.

"Now I know where we are!" Nancy exclaimed jubilantly. "We're near the front boundary wall."

A few hundred feet farther on they saw the wall itself and scrambled over it. The trio reached the shelter of the car just as the first raindrops splashed against the windshield. Fortunately Nancy was able to drive to the paved highway before the side road became a mire of mud.

She dropped the cousins at their houses, then went home. Over a late lunch of milk and a sandwich, she thought about the mystery.

"I might get some kind of a lead from Walter Heath's will," she decided, "and I'd like to find out where Juliana did her banking. There might be a clue in the last withdrawals."

Nancy called Lieutenant Masters. "The police couldn't locate any bank accounts," the officer told her. "A very large sum of money was found in Juliana's apartment in New York. But she had several bills from stores, and by the time they were paid from this cash, there was nothing left."

"Then that's a dead end," said Nancy. "How about the will?"

"I don't know," said the officer. She agreed to meet Nancy the next morning at the courthouse to examine the document. Daniel Hector was named as sole executor.

A quick reading confirmed what Mrs. Fenimore had told her. The entire Heath estate had been bequeathed to Juliana Johnson on the condition that she claim it within five years of Walter Heath's death.

One clause in the will held Nancy's attention. It read:

"It is my belief and hope that Juliana still lives and will claim the property within the allotted time. She will be able to identify herself in a special way, thus insuring that no impostor can receive my estate."

"I wonder what that means," Nancy mused.

"I haven't any idea," Lieutenant Masters said.

They went over the document again, but it gave no clue to the way in which Juliana might establish her identity.

"I must find out what Mr. Heath meant by this," said Nancy. "Obviously it's a very important clue!"

CHAPTER V

Suspicious Figures

NANCY suggested to Lieutenant Masters that they go at once to see Mrs. Fenimore. "She may know by what special means Walter Heath expected Juliana to identify herself."

The young officer agreed. She and Nancy drove to the Fenimore house in their own cars. They found the woman seated in the living room.

"Good morning," Mrs. Fenimore, who seemed to be feeling better, greeted the visitors warmly. She stared anxiously at the policewoman. "It's— it's not Joan again?"

"No. In fact, my two rosebushes have been returned. We came to ask you a few more questions about your sister," Nancy replied.

The woman relaxed but spoke wearily. "I'll tell you everything I can. A couple of years ago I gave up hope that she would be found, but I've never told Joan this."

"Then you believe that your sister may not be living?" Nancy asked soberly.

"Oh no. I'm sure Julie is alive," Mrs. Fenimore replied, "but I'm afraid she may have disappeared for good, and I'll never see her again."

"Would you give us some personal information about your sister?" Lieutenant Masters asked kindly. "Was she younger than you?"

"No. Julie was seven years older. Our parents died when we were children, and we lived with an aunt who was pretty strict. I never minded Aunt Mattie's scolding, but Julie, who was high strung, resented it. She took dancing lessons secretly, and when Aunt Mattie found out and punished her for it, Julie ran away.

"For several years Julie danced wherever she could get an engagement and studied during her spare moments."

The policewoman asked, "Did you see Juliana often after she became famous?"

"Only now and then. But she called me every week. I was so excited when she became engaged to Walter Heath. It was to be kept from the press, so of course I told no one."

"Could anything have happened between Juliana and Mr. Heath to make her unhappy enough to disappear?" Nancy asked.

Mrs. Fenimore shook her head. "Julie was beautiful and talented. He was handsome, wealthy, and kind. They adored each other. I'm sure he had nothing to do with her disappearance."

Mention of the deceased estate owner reminded Nancy of the real purpose of her call. She asked Mrs. Fenimore about the strange identification clause in the will.

"I wondered myself what that meant when I read it," the woman replied.

"Do you think Daniel Hector might have an answer?" Nancy asked.

Mrs. Fenimore's face darkened. "Please don't mention that man's name! I detest him. All these years he's only been pretending to search for Julie."

"Pretending?"

"Once in a while he would call to tell me about his attempts to find her but they sounded half-hearted. Now he doesn't even phone. I'm sure he's stopped trying. I'm counting on you, Nancy, to solve the mystery."

Nancy promised to do everything she could to trace the missing dancer. Secretly she wondered if she could find the woman in time to save the inheritance for her.

"May I see a photograph of your sister?" she requested.

"I have a number of excellent ones," Mrs. Fenimore replied. "I'll give you one. They're in the drawer of this table."

She took them out. There were six, taken years

before when the dancer was at the height of her career. Several were inscribed with her name and a greeting. The face was a distinctive one. Carefully Nancy noted the perfect features, the beautiful dark eyes, the straight nose and firm chin.

"Julie may have changed a great deal since I last saw her," Mrs. Fenimore remarked. "Ten years have gone by."

"Your sister is lovely," Nancy commented. "Joan looks a little like her."

"Yes, she does. And certainly my daughter has Julie's vivacious ways. She's quite a little actress. Maybe someday—"

Mrs. Fenimore looked sadly into space. Lieutenant Masters, fearing the conversation had upset the woman, said they must leave.

"Please try not to worry," Nancy urged Mrs. Fenimore who handed her a photograph as they said good-by.

When she and the officer reached their cars, Nancy thanked Lieutenant Masters for her help.

"Call on me any time," the young woman said as she drove off.

Nancy decided to take a walk and think about the case.

As she wandered up the street, children were coming home from school to lunch. She saw Joan playing with an older boy in a vacant lot. They were tossing a ball for a dog to retrieve.

"That boy looks familiar," Nancy thought as she walked over to the children. Suddenly, in a fit of temper, the boy hit the dog with a stick.

"Cut it out!" he shouted. "You're chewing my ball to pieces!"

Joan screamed.

"Stop that!" Nancy ordered. "The dog hasn't hurt your ball. He was only playing."

The boy gazed at her with hard, unfriendly eyes. "Is he your dog?" he asked impudently.

"No."

"Then it's none of your business if I hit him."

Nancy started to reply, but it was not necessary. The dog dropped the ball and slunk off. The boy picked it up. Then, giving Nancy a baleful look, he ran away.

Nancy took Joan by the hand and led her off. As tactfully as possible she suggested that the child ought to find a girl playmate.

"Teddy Hooper's okay. He's the only one that lives close to me," Joan replied, skipping happily along beside her companion. "I don't like him when he's mean, but most of the time he's a lot of fun. He always thinks up exciting things to do."

"You'd better hurry home to lunch," Nancy said. "I'll go with you. My car's there."

When they reached the house, Joan hugged Nancy, then ran inside. Nancy was sure she had made a firm friend of the little girl.

"I'm not far from Salty's," the young detec-

"Stop that!" Nancy ordered.

tive said to herself. "I'll drive there and find out if he has seen that man who crashed into our boat."

In a little while she came to the clam digger's home. The sailor was on the shore repairing his rowboat.

"Well, now, me lass, I'm glad to see you," he said. "But I'm afraid I haven't got good news."

"You mean about the boat?"

"I've looked high an' low for that damaged boat," the man said regretfully. "It's not tied up anywhere along here."

"How about Harper's Inlet?" Nancy asked.

Salty admitted he had not been there. "Too busy," he explained. "Maybe I'll go this afternoon. I need a mess o' clams an' there be some up the inlet. You want to come along? I'll show you the Heath factory."

For Nancy the opportunity was too good to pass up. She was eager to visit the spot.

"Just tell me when to be here," she said.

After settling on three o'clock, she remarked, "I'll bring along one of my friends."

Nancy hurried home for a quick lunch, then telephoned George. Promptly at three o'clock the two girls met Salty at the waterfront.

"I'll put ye to work," the sailor chuckled as he gathered together his fishing and clamming equipment. "Help me load these into the rowboat, will you?"

The old man's muscular arms rippled as he dug the oars into the tranquil waters of the Muskoka River. Presently he and his passengers were skimming along at a rapid rate. Behind the craft trailed a long copper wire which gleamed in the sunlight.

"I'm trollin' for my dinner tonight," Salty explained. "There's somethin' yankin' on my line right now, I do believe!"

He rested the oars and pulled in the line. Finally a four-pound speckled bass flopped into the boat.

"She's a beauty," he said, grinning.

While the girls kept the craft from drifting downstream, Salty removed the hook from the fish and dropped his catch into a woven basket. Then he wound up the copper troll line and put it away.

"Fishin's not much good in the inlet," he remarked. "But we'll find clams."

The upper river was very still. As the boat entered Harper's Inlet some time later, there was no sound except the occasional chirping of a bird. Nancy hunched low now and then, to avoid the overhanging bushes and watched the coves for a hidden boat. There was none.

"It doesn't look as if we're goin' to find your friend," Salty remarked after he had rowed a quarter of a mile upstream. "We're almost to Heath's button factory now. I'll anchor here."

The man had located a bed of clams in the shallow water. He asked the girls to balance his fish basket on the gunwale, then waded in to dig the clams from the mud and sand with his rake. As he tossed them, one by one, he kept singing snatches of familiar sea songs.

"Basket's full," Nancy called several minutes later.

Salty got into the boat and started off again. As they rounded a bend, the girls saw a large, square building set some distance back from the shore. The banks nearby were littered with discarded bits of clamshells.

"That's the Heath button factory," Salty said. "She's sure gone to pieces."

Nancy gazed curiously at the neglected brick structure. Vines which had grown up the building's walls lay thick on the shingle roof and all the windows were broken.

Suddenly Nancy spotted two figures near the factory entrance. As they vanished into the building, Salty pointed to an object hidden near some bushes.

"A boat!" he exclaimed. "And her prow's damaged, too!"

The bow of the boat had been drawn up on the sand. Nancy and George recognized it immediately as the blue-and-white craft that had struck them!

"Oh, Salty, please pull in here!" Nancy begged.

As he did, she told him about the men.

"Humph!" Salty grunted. "I'll bet ye a mess o' clams they ain't got no right in there!"

Nancy nodded. "I want to talk to them. Will you stay here near the damaged boat? If the men come out, try to hold them until we get back."

The sailor did not like being left out of the search, but before he could protest, the girls were splashing through knee-deep water to shore.

CHAPTER VI

A Mysterious Explosion

NANCY and George had to cross a stretch of low, marshy land in order to reach the old button factory. Their sneakers, already water-soaked, became caked with mud. The girls were grateful for the high wild grass that screened their approach.

"You know," Nancy said, "those two men looked familiar."

"Who are they?"

"I'm not sure, but one of them was thin and wore a blue cap like the fellow who crashed into our motorboat. The other resembled Daniel Hector, the lawyer."

While still twenty yards from the factory, the girls were startled to hear the sound of hammering. The pounding noise came from inside the building.

"I wonder what those men are doing in there,"

Nancy said, cautiously pulling aside the tall vines.

"Maybe they're workmen who were sent to repair the place," George replied.

Nancy offered no comment. It was possible that Daniel Hector had brought another man to the property either to inspect it, or to do some work. But she seriously doubted this.

As the girls moved closer, the hammering ceased. Though they waited several minutes, it did not resume.

"We may have been seen by the men," Nancy said. "I hope they haven't left."

When George and Nancy had pushed through to the end of the marsh, they saw that the front door to the factory stood wide open. Nancy peered inside. A long corridor opened into several offices and led to a large workroom at the rear. No one was in sight.

As the girls started along the hallway, they heard retreating footsteps. They glanced out a dirt-smudged window and noticed two men running in the direction of the river.

"Oh, Nancy," George exclaimed, "they must have heard us!"

"They're going to their boat!" Nancy said excitedly.

Already the men were well hidden by the high marsh grass. The girls ran quickly toward a rear door, with Nancy far in the lead. As they neared it, deafening sounds of an explosion filled the air. The walls of the factory rocked. A huge amount of plaster crashed down between the girls.

"Nancy!" George cried out in panic as she gazed at the high pile of debris that separated them. One whole corridor wall had caved in.

"Nancy must be buried underneath it!" George thought in horror.

The air was thick with white dust. Coughing and choking, George frantically began to pull away boards and chunks of plaster.

In the meantime the two men, who had paused in the tall grass, were just about to go back to the factory when they heard someone running up the path. Salty, fearful for the girls' safety, was racing toward the building, clam rake over his shoulder. He passed within a few feet of the men, but did not see them.

"Oh dear! Oh dear!" he kept mumbling. "I hope nothin's happened to the lassies!"

He found George still digging feverishly at the pile of debris.

"Salty!" the girl cried. "I can't find Nancy! She must be buried!"

The old man began raking furiously at the pile of plaster that blocked the corridor. At that moment Nancy was lying stunned on the floor of a closet some distance from where her friends were working. The force of the explosion had hurled her into the large storage closet, then the door had slammed shut. The corridor ceiling had fallen, sealing off the entrance to the closet.

When she regained consciousness Nancy found herself in total darkness and wondered where she was. Slowly the dazed girl got to her feet and felt around her prison. At last she found a door and tried it. It would not budge, and there was no other exit.

"What'll I do?" she thought. "And where is George?"

Suddenly Nancy heard her name being called. With all her strength she pushed against the door. It yielded slightly. Through the crack she shouted, "George!"

"Nancy! Where are you?" came a muffled reply.

"Here! In the closet!"

Salty and George leaped across the rubble. With the rake and their hands and feet they cleared away enough of the debris to free Nancy. As she squeezed outside, Salty mumbled:

"Thank goodness you're alive!"

George embraced her friend in excited relief. "You feel all right?"

"I think so. What caused the explosion?"

Suddenly Nancy recalled the two men who had run from the building. "What became of those men who were in here? Did you see them, Salty?"

The clam digger shook his head. "I saw no one."

Nancy, George, and Salty plunged through the

marsh grass toward the riverbank. The damaged motorboat was no longer there.

"Those rascals sneaked away, drat 'em!" Salty muttered in disgust. "Do you think that makes 'em guilty, Nancy?"

"Guilty on two counts," the girl replied. "Guilty of damaging the boat I rented, and most likely, guilty of causing the explosion."

"But why set off an explosion?" George asked.

Nancy shrugged. She did not want to mention any of her theories just yet, but it occurred to her that Daniel Hector may have been covering up some incriminating evidence against himself. Mrs. Fenimore had vehemently declared that she did not trust the lawyer.

During the trip back to Salty's dock, the clam digger and the girls kept their eyes open for the blue-and-white motorboat. But they did not see it.

"I'll be glad to take ye on a trip again," the amiable man offered when they reached River Heights.

Nancy thanked him. On the way home she was thoughtful, and could hardly wait for the moment when she could talk to her father. In his den after dinner she told about Daniel Hector's apparent connection with the explosion at the Heath button factory.

"But why would Hector want to damage property he's obligated to look after?" Mr. Drew asked. "It doesn't make sense."

"I'm sure there's a great deal more to the Heath case than Juliana's disappearance," Nancy declared. "The explosion today, for example. There may be something pretty sinister in back of it all."

"I agree with you," Mr. Drew said soberly. "Nancy, I know it's useless to ask you to give up trying to solve a mystery—"

"Oh, it is, Dad!"

"At least I can ask you to be careful. Remember, you're my one and only daughter."

"I'll keep it in mind," she said, hugging him affectionately. "Now, about the Heath affair. Isn't it possible that Hector has been investigating the property himself, hoping to discover the clue Walter Heath mentioned in his will?"

"You mean the one by which Juliana can identify herself beyond all doubt?"

"Yes, Dad. If a dishonest person stumbled upon that clue, it might be possible for him to have an impostor claim the fortune."

"That wouldn't be so easy, Nancy. A number of persons knew Juliana."

"But," Nancy countered, "if she has been through a terrible experience of some kind, she could have changed so much even her own sister wouldn't recognize her."

"True. I follow your reasoning. Nevertheless, any woman who put in a claim would have to satisfy the court that it was a just one."

Nancy glanced steadily at her father. "Do you

think Mr. Hector has really tried to find Juliana?
If he isn't honest—"

"Nancy, I don't like to think the man would be
involved in anything underhanded. I don't ap-
prove of his methods in handling law cases, but
there is no proof that he has actually done anything dishonest."

"But you admit," Nancy said, "that the Heath
case looks suspicious?"

"Yes, I do, Nancy."

His daughter went on, "I've even thought that
maybe Juliana is being held a prisoner somewhere."

Mr. Drew looked surprised. "In the castle?"

"Who knows?" Nancy replied. "Dad, I can't
decide where to begin looking for her. The explosion today kind of changed my plans."

"In what way?"

"I heard that Walter Heath made scientific experiments at his estate. If Mr. Hector suspects
there's a secret within those crumbling walls—"

Mr. Drew gazed at Nancy. "Young lady, you're
leading up to something!" he declared with a
twinkle in his eye. "Out with it!"

"I'm only trying to arouse your curiosity,"
Nancy confessed with a laugh. "Why not go to the
factory with me? You may find a clue I over-
looked. I need your help, Dad."

"Well, if you put it that way," her father said,

"Actually, I haven't the time to spare, but I'll go to please you."

"Tomorrow morning then."

"So soon?"

"Dad, don't forget, I must solve this mystery in three weeks!"

CHAPTER VII

A Puzzling Message

NANCY and her father were up early the next morning. They hastily made breakfast before Hannah came downstairs, then drove to the lane Mr. Drew knew led to the damaged button factory. The road was in very bad condition, and there was no gate.

"I see why those men came by boat," said Mr. Drew, stopping the car some distance from the building. "We'll walk from here."

Nancy led the way through the dew-laden grass to the scene of the explosion. There was no sign of anyone near the factory.

"The explosion did a good job of destruction," the lawyer commented as the Drews cautiously entered the building.

"Here's where the wall caved in between George and me," Nancy explained.

"Looks as if it might have been dynamited,"

her father remarked. "Let's see if we can find any evidence."

For the next half hour father and daughter scrambled among the rubble. When they discovered nothing of importance in the corridor, they decided to investigate the large workroom at the rear. It was necessary to go outside and climb in through a window to reach the room, because the inside entrance was blocked.

"Oh, it's like a ghost town," Nancy said as she surveyed the rusted machinery covered with layers of dust. "To think that this once was a prosperous factory, Dad." She pointed. "What was this machine used for?"

"Cutting," her father explained. "The mollusk shell is placed inside. An operator moves a lever and down comes the circular steel saw. Presto! A little shell disk drops into the hopper. Another machine slices the disk into pieces of uniform thickness and there you have some pearl buttons!"

"How clever!" said Nancy.

"The buttons pass through still another machine which polishes them," Mr. Drew went on. "In the last operation thread holes are drilled through them."

"Dad! Look!" Nancy cried suddenly.

A scrap of torn paper was sticking from a corner of the rubble in the doorway. Near it, in a thick layer of dust, were several footprints.

Nancy picked up the paper which had part of a message on it. The writing was bold and read:

> Dear C,
>   Some
> cret which I
> in a wall
> famous
> worthy

"Interesting," Mr. Drew commented, scanning the paper. "But I can't say that it makes much sense. The footprints might be a better clue."

He stooped to examine them. "Freshly made, no doubt," he said. "Perhaps the two men have visited here since the explosion."

"If so, it proves they're searching for something they think was hidden and could be found only by blasting it out."

"Not necessarily. The explosion could have been an accident, or was set off for some other purpose and may have nothing to do with Juliana's inheritance," Mr. Drew remarked.

Nancy was staring at the torn note. "I believe I've stumbled upon a worthwhile clue just the same. I'm sure the partially missing word is *secret*."

She pocketed the message and reluctantly left the factory with her father. At home, later on, Nancy spent more than an hour trying to figure out the missing words of the note. Who had written them? The paper appeared old, the ink slightly faded.

"It wouldn't surprise me if Walter Heath had written this," she told Hannah Gruen.

"I know how you might find out!" the housekeeper said.

"How?"

"Walter Heath was a member of the River Heights Historical Society before his death. I'm sure the society has specimens of his handwriting."

"Hannah, you're a genius!" Nancy cried, giving the woman a hug. "I'm off to the Historical Society this very minute!"

Luck was with the young detective. On labels, books, and pieces of furniture which Walter Heath had given to the organization's museum she found several samples of the deceased estate owner's handwriting.

"It's the same as that in the note!" Nancy observed excitedly. "Now, if only I can find the missing part of the message! But Daniel Hector may have the rest!"

Nancy decided to seek her father's aid once more and asked him to talk to the lawyer about the Heath case. Carson Drew did, and then reported to his daughter. "Hector certainly was reluctant to discuss the case."

"Didn't he tell you anything?" Nancy asked.

"Nothing worth mentioning. As soon as I spoke of Heath Castle and the button factory, he closed up as tight as Salty's clams!"

"Did you mention Juliana's name?"

"Yes. Mr. Hector stressed that he was still searching for her."

The Heath Castle mystery was no nearer a solution than before. Eager as Nancy was to revisit the estate that afternoon, she found it impossible. Her father had made her promise not to go there alone. Neither Bess nor George was free to accompany her until the next day.

The next day, after Sunday church services, the three girls set out in Nancy's car, carrying a picnic lunch. On the way Nancy explained the latest developments in the mystery. She added, "Nothing must drive us away from the castle grounds until we've investigated every nook and corner!"

Soon the familiar ivy-covered front boundary wall loomed ahead. Nancy parked beneath a cool tunnel of overhanging trees. The car was well hidden.

She and her friends got out and walked to the rusty gate and peered between the bars. The grounds seemed as deserted as ever, but suddenly the girls heard dogs barking.

"Listen!" Nancy exclaimed. An instant later she added, "They're inside the grounds!"

"And coming closer," Bess said nervously.

"That settles it. We can't possibly go in now!"

She wanted to return to the car, but George and Nancy lingered, reluctant to leave. Soon they glimpsed two large black-and-white hounds.

"Dangerous-looking brutes," George commented. "Evidently they've been left here on guard."

When the dogs saw the intruders they barked louder than ever. One of them came to the gate, growled fiercely at Nancy, and clawed the iron bars with his front paws.

Instead of retreating, she spoke soothingly to him. "Hello, old fellow. When did you come to live here?"

To the amazement of Bess, the animal began to wag his tail. Nancy reached a hand through the gate and patted his head.

"Be careful!" Bess warned sharply.

The other dog had stopped barking and now came forward, too. Nancy stroked his head.

"These dogs are not vicious," she said. "Girls, I'm sure we can explore the grounds safely."

"I'm willing to try if you are," George said.

Bess was afraid of the dogs but agreed to go.

"I'll climb over first," Nancy said. "If they don't attack me, you two follow."

George and Bess watched uneasily as their friend climbed the crumbling wall. On the ledge she hesitated a moment. The dogs had set up a loud barking again. Nancy realized that although the animals had been friendly to her on the opposite side of the enclosure, there was no guarantee they would let her enter the grounds.

"Don't attempt it!" Bess called.

Nancy spoke gently but firmly to the hounds. Then, taking a chance, she lowered herself gradually. One of the dogs leaped up to her. Nancy's heart began to beat wildly, but she showed no fear.

"Easy, boy," she murmured. To her relief, the animal became friendly once more.

"It's all right," Nancy called to her friends, and continued to pat the hounds. She talked to them as George climbed the wall and leaped down. The dogs did not make a fuss. As soon as Bess's head appeared, however, they began to snarl.

"They'll leave you alone if you don't show any fear," Nancy assured her.

But it was impossible for Bess to do this. "Go on without me," she said after two vain attempts. "I'll wait in the car."

"All right," Nancy agreed, adding with a grin, "Don't eat up all the lunch while we're gone!"

She and George set off. The dogs remained behind. Soon the girls located the avenue of trees which led to the loggia.

"Here's a path that may go to the castle," Nancy said as they came to a forked trail.

"Maybe." George smiled. "But here's a sign that reads *To the Goblin Gallery*."

"Let's see where it goes," Nancy urged.

They passed a finely chiseled statuette in a wall niche, lingered a moment to gaze at a rose garden choked with weeds, then went on to a clearing. Before them rose an artistic structure. The sides were formed of slender twisted stone columns, while sprawling over them was a roof of un-trimmed vines supported by thick stalks.

"How pretty!" Nancy said dreamily.

George, surveying the gallery closely, remarked practically, "It looks as if Father Time has taken over here instead of the goblins. Those stone columns might tumble down any minute."

Remarking that she was amazed stone could be damaged so greatly by weather, Nancy stooped to inspect the base of one of the pillars. "George!" she exclaimed suddenly. "Someone has deliber-ately tampered with these columns. See the marks? They've been weakened—probably with a pickax!"

"Why would anyone do that?" George asked.

As the girls looked over the other columns, Nancy told George about the note she had found at the Heath button factory and the words "in a wall."

"I'm sure someone is searching various walls of that old building for an article of value," she said.

"But why try to destroy these lovely columns?"

"Maybe the person didn't find what he wanted in the walls, and was looking in the columns."

George was not listening attentively to her friend. Instead, she was gazing down the path as if transfixed.

"What do you see?" Nancy asked in a low voice.

George motioned toward the bushes. "It's an old man!" she whispered. "He's pointing his finger at something ahead of us!"

Nancy was startled too when she saw the man amid the heavy shrubbery. Her pulse quickened as she moved toward the figure. Nearing it, she laughed softly.

"Why, it's only a life-size statue, George!"

Embarrassed, her friend went over to inspect the figure.

"That pointing finger might have a special significance," Nancy said, noting the path ahead. "Let's see where this takes us."

The trail had been nearly obliterated by weeds. It twisted in and out among the trees and seemed to lead nowhere. The girls were about to turn back when Nancy caught a flash of water in sunlight.

The girls made their way through the undergrowth and came out on the shore of a very large pond dotted with rank grass. George hurried ahead to look at it.

"Why do you suppose someone pointed the statue to this? It doesn't look like any—"

Her words ended in a little scream as the soft bank beneath her feet gave way. Before Nancy could grab her, George had slipped into the water. It was not deep but she was soaked.

"Hypers! Look at me! I'm a mess!" George cried out. "And say, this water is kind of salty."

Nancy helped her friend scramble up the slippery bank. She gazed about her and noticed a stone house nearby. Apparently it once had been used as a tool shed.

"Go in there and get out of your wet clothes," she advised George. "I'll lay them in the sun. They shouldn't take long to dry."

Quickly George ducked into the stone house. She tossed her slacks, shirt, and sneakers through an open window.

Nancy spread them on the bank in the sun, then started walking around the pond. Suddenly she noticed something shiny on the bank. It was the shell of a whelk.

"How beautiful!" she thought, picking it up. The mother-of-pearl lining gleamed with a blend of delicate pink and purple.

After a moment's hesitation Nancy stripped off shoes and socks and waded into the shallow water. When she dipped her hands into the sand, she discovered that the bottom was thick with mussels. Among them were discarded shells with the same lovely blending of colors. Nearby on the shore she spotted a large pile of cracked shells and went to examine them.

"Why are they here?" she wondered. "These

are seashore whelks." Then Nancy remembered what Salty had told her about dye being obtained from this type of shellfish and that Walter Heath had spent much of his time on scientific experiments. "Suppose he was using the whelks to make a special kind of dye!"

Nancy tucked two unbroken shells into her shirt pocket. As she put on her shoes she thought of the hacked stone columns and the explosion at the factory. "Someone may be looking for a secret connected with Walter Heath's experiments!"

"Nancy!" George called. "Are my clothes dry?"

Nancy rose and felt them. "Not yet."

"I'm getting hungry," George complained. "And Bess will have a fit if we don't go back soon."

At that moment Bess was fuming in Nancy's concealed car. As the sun climbed high overhead and the girls failed to return, she became hungry and annoyed.

"Guess they've forgotten me," she thought. To add to her irritation, the hounds would dash back to the gate whenever she walked over to look through it. They bayed savagely.

"Oh," Bess fretted, "wait until I see Nancy and George. I'll—"

Just then she heard a car coming up the road. Bess barely had time to hide herself in the bushes before it swung around the bend. She was glad that she had followed her instinct for she was sure from Nancy's description that the driver was Daniel Hector. He was alone.

The lawyer stopped in front of the gate but did not shut off the engine. He got out of his two-door car, leaving the door on his side open.

"He's going to drive into the grounds!" Bess thought. "Nancy and George will be caught! I must warn them!"

Her anxiety mounting, Bess tried to think what to do. Mr. Hector still had his back turned toward her as he unlocked the big gates. The car was less than ten feet away from her hiding place.

There was little time for Bess to think or plan. Impulsively she darted to the car. After climbing into the back, she crouched on the floor.

Hector returned to the automobile. Unaware of his passenger, he drove through the opening into the estate grounds!

CHAPTER VIII

Locked In!

"GEORGE, would you mind if I do a little exploring?" Nancy asked. "I'll be back by the time your clothes are dry."

"Okay," George called.

"I'm not going far. I've found some whelk shells, and I think they may indicate something important. Maybe dye made from them is hidden in containers nearby."

"They're not in here," George said.

Nancy moved off, looking about carefully for any possible place where dye might have been stored. She found none, and in her search wandered farther than she had intended.

Nancy paused abruptly as she became aware of a low rumble which shook the earth. "What's that?" she wondered.

She stood still and waited for more sounds, but there were none. In the distance, however, a cloud of white, powdery dust caught her attention.

"Another explosion!" she murmured excitedly. Cautiously Nancy went toward the area, but soon her path was blocked by a high brier hedge.

After following the bushes some distance to find an opening, the young detective was startled to hear a car.

"Somebody with a key to the gate padlock must have driven into the estate grounds!" she thought.

As the sound drew nearer, Nancy decided to find out who was coming. She plunged through the woodland and reached a weed-grown clearing just as Daniel Hector drove up and stopped.

Nancy backed quickly into the shelter of the bushes. The lawyer did not see her. He parked his car under a gnarled maple, got out, and set off on foot.

"I'll follow him," Nancy decided.

Mr. Hector walked so fast that she could scarcely keep him in sight. He seemed thoroughly acquainted with the layout of the trails, for he never hesitated when he came to a turn.

Before long the man vanished from view. When Nancy came to a fork in the path, she wondered which way he had gone. Fearful she would lose track of him entirely, Nancy pressed her ear to the ground and very faintly could discern a steady beat to her right. She hastened on.

Presently the trail branched off in three directions. Again Nancy was baffled. When she flattened herself on the ground this time, she could hear nothing.

"I've lost him!" she thought in dismay.

Nancy chose a path at random and went on doggedly. She was so intent on her sleuthing she completely forgot about George and Bess.

Meanwhile Bess, still hidden in Daniel Hector's car, was wondering what to do. "I'd better find George and Nancy," she decided.

She cautiously climbed out and started up the trail the lawyer had taken. Bess had not gone far when the dogs began to bark. They were coming closer each moment!

"They've picked up my scent!" Bess was in a panic.

The hounds leaped into view. In terror, Bess shinned up a tree and hoped the dogs would pass by. Instead they took up a vigil at the base of the trunk.

By this time George had grown tired of waiting for Nancy to return to the tool house. From the window she could see her clothes, apparently dry, on the sunny bank of the pond.

"I can't wait another minute!" she thought impatiently. "I'll get them myself!"

George went to the door and stopped short. A boy in faded overalls had emerged from among the trees. He seemed to be eleven or twelve years old.

George slipped out of sight behind the door

and watched him. He suddenly snatched up her clothes and hurried off.

"Hey, you! Those are mine!" George cried angrily from the window.

The boy paid no attention.

"Hypers!" George thought in despair. "Now what'll I do? Nancy's done a disappearing act, and I'm stranded here without any clothes!"

Nancy, unaware of her friends' problems, was intent on another subject. The trail she had chosen had not led her to Daniel Hector, but to Heath Castle. She could not resist the temptation to see the wonderful building at close range.

Its beauty, even at a distance, awed her. It was constructed of massive gray stone covered with ivy. The roof line was broken by several turrets, a large one at each end of the residence, with smaller ones in between.

"It's a perfect copy of an old English castle," Nancy thought, "only smaller."

Curious, she began to circle the castle walls. "What a pity this stately home has to stand in the midst of ruined gardens!" she mused.

A massive side door of the big house stood ajar. Nancy wondered if Mr. Hector had opened it. Quietly she slipped inside.

She found herself in a long corridor which twisted and turned crazily. Large rooms lined with beautiful paneled wood opened from it. Many were empty, others contained a few pieces of fine old mahogany furniture. At a glance it was apparent to Nancy that nearly everything of value had been removed from the place.

"Odd," she said to herself. "I thought the castle was left to Juliana intact. Did thieves break in or did Hector sell the furniture?"

The inside wooden shutters in the gloomy rooms were closed, lending a ghostly appearance to the few sheet-draped chairs. The unexpected sight of herself in a long mirror gave Nancy a start.

Before long she found steps leading to the second floor. A search of the rooms there, including the many closets, revealed nothing of special interest.

"The only places left to visit are the towers," Nancy thought. "But how do I get into them?"

She could locate no entrance. Then, glancing from a window, she realized that the castle was built around a hollow square which was another tangled garden. Nancy figured that some of the smaller turrets actually were bedrooms. The high towers must be separate, with doors opening from the courtyard.

Nancy hurried down the stairway to hunt for an exit to the inner garden. At length she found a door in the shadows of the corridor. After tripping the bolt so she would not lock herself out, Nancy stepped into the sunshine.

She glanced around and discovered that her

guess had been right. There were entrance doors to the two high, round towers. She opened the one on her left. It held one room which had a low ceiling and contained nothing. The walls, however, had been chipped and damaged.

"Even the castle hasn't escaped the hackers!" Nancy mused. She turned her attention to the other tower, glad that the massive door to it was unlocked. It was hollow and only dimly lighted by a high window. A circular iron stairway led to a small balcony at the top.

Nancy looked around on the ground floor but saw nothing of interest. She climbed up and found a little door at the head of the stairway. Cautiously pushing on it, she peered beyond.

As her eyes became accustomed to the somber light, she saw that there was nothing in the tiny room, nor on the open parapet beyond it. In disappointment, Nancy leaned on the wide rail.

"All this work just to get a view," she thought. "But at least I have an idea of the layout."

Suddenly her attention focused on a figure running far in the distance. A boy had moved toward the wall and was carrying a bundle under his arm. Just before he disappeared from sight behind tall trees, he dropped something. It looked like a pair of slacks.

"Oh, my goodness!" Nancy thought with a fearful pang of conscience. "Maybe he stole George's clothes! I should never have left her alone at the tool house. And the boy looked like Teddy Hooper!"

The youngster appeared again, but this time outside the walls, running across the beach toward a boat. "There must be a way out besides the main gate," Nancy thought. Since the boy was much too far away for her to call him, she quickly retraced her steps to the courtyard door below.

When she tried to pull it open, the door would not budge. She yanked and yanked. Finally she realized that somebody must have locked it! She tried the key she had to the castle, but it did not fit.

She was a prisoner in the tower!

"Oh, I must get out!" she murmured.

Nancy refused to panic and told herself there must be some way to escape! She returned to the open parapet and looked about. It was a forty-foot drop to the ground and there was no possible way to climb down the tower wall.

Thoroughly discouraged, Nancy went to try the locked door again. As she twisted the knob vainly, she heard voices. Her heart leaped! Two men were outside.

"We'll get caught, I tell you!" one was arguing in a loud voice. "And if we do, the old man'll say he never saw us before!"

Nancy wondered if "the old man" might be Hector.

"Oh, quit worrying," the other man growled. "Just leave the brainwork of this job to me. We'll find that clue yet. It's somewhere in one of the walls of the estate."

"Yeah? Which wall?" the first man asked sarcastically. "The place is full of them. Anyhow, I'm satisfied with what we've found and kept."

"When he sees all the walls we've blasted, he can't say we didn't do a pretty thorough job for him." The other snickered.

The voices faded out, and Nancy assumed that the two speakers had moved away. Who were they? Their voices had been unfamiliar.

"Well, a few of my theories are confirmed, anyway," Nancy said to herself. "The walls of Heath Castle and the gardens have been damaged deliberately, and on orders from a person who wants to find a valuable secret."

Nancy hoped to catch a glimpse of the men and returned to the parapet. She did not see them, but a moment later heard them whistling and calling to the dogs. Then all became quiet.

"They've gone," Nancy thought in relief. "Maybe I should have let them know I was in here when I had the chance. But no, they're not honest, and they probably would have ruined all my plans. I'll get out somehow!"

Nancy was in a predicament, nevertheless. George, stranded without clothes at the tool house, could not help her. Bess, she assumed, was still waiting in the parked car outside the castle gate.

Nancy roved restlessly about the ground floor of the tower in her vain search for an exit. Looking at her watch for the first time, the imprisoned girl was amazed to discover that it was after four o'clock—and she was hungry!

"By this time Bess and George must be pretty annoyed with me," she thought guiltily.

While Nancy worried, Bess was perched in a tree a considerable distance from the castle. Surrounded by the watchful dogs, she would not descend for fear they might tear her to pieces!

Badly shaken and near tears, she suddenly heard a whistle. The dogs pricked up their ears, then raced away.

"Thank goodness," Bess gasped, sliding down from her leafy prison.

So much time had elapsed she decided it would do no good to look for Nancy and George. If they had not encountered Mr. Hector already, they surely would have returned to the car.

"I'll go back there," Bess concluded. "But which way?"

Hopelessly confused, she started off. After a while Bess came to the estate wall. Just ahead of her she noticed something in the grass.

"George's slacks!" Bess thought with a start.

There was no sign of either her cousin or Nancy. Bess could not believe that they had gone for a swim. As she picked up the slacks, she wondered apprehensively what had happened.

"This path seems to run along the wall," Bess said to herself. "If I take it, I should get back to the gate eventually."

But she found that the trail changed direction. Instead of the main gate she reached a large pond.

"Oh, where am I?" Bess fretted desperately.

Suddenly she heard her name called. She whirled around. No one was in sight. A few yards away stood a stone tool house, its window hidden by overhanging branches.

"Bess!" George shouted impatiently. "Over here! I'm in the tool house!"

Bess hastened to the small building and looked inside.

"I've been stranded here for hours!" George fumed.

"How did you lose your clothes?"

"I fell into the water and took them off to dry. Nancy put them on the bank. Then she went off to do some exploring. A boy came along and ran away with my things!"

"How terrible! What became of Nancy?"

"I wish I knew. She's been gone a long while. But tell me, how did you get up your courage to climb the wall?"

When Bess told of her secret ride with Hector, George burst into laughter despite her worry about Nancy.

Then she sobered. "Hector is on the grounds! Maybe Nancy ran into him!"

The cousins were not sure what they should do. Finally Bess said, "Let's go back to the car. Nancy might be there."

"How can I go anywhere like this?" George cried.

Bess handed the girl her slacks. "I found these by the wall. The boy must have dropped them. And you can wear my sweater. I'll be warm enough in my blouse."

George put on the clothes and was relieved to find her sneakers still lying near the bank of the pond. The girls hurried off.

Without meeting anyone, or being attacked by the dogs, they managed to find their way to the front wall and climbed over. Nancy was not in the car.

"Let's drive to town and get help," Bess said.

"Nancy has the car keys!"

"Oh, I'd forgotten. Well, we are in an awful mess!"

"We'll have to find Nancy, that's all there is to it," Bess declared.

Each of the girls ate a sandwich from the picnic lunch, then started to scale the wall again. On the ledge they hesitated. The dogs had come back and began to growl fiercely.

"Maybe if we feed them—" George said. She got the rest of the sandwiches from the car. At the sight of the food the hounds became friendly, but the instant they had gobbled it up, they lay down on the ground, panting. Again and again George tried to descend, but each time the dogs rose menacingly.

Bess would not even try to re-enter the grounds. "It's no use," she said.

"I suppose you're right," George said, and jumped down on the outside.

"Tell you what," Bess said. "You stay here and I'll go for help!"

CHAPTER IX

Trap Door

FOR hours Nancy had refused to acknowledge that there was no means of escape from the tower. She had pried at the lock with a nail file from her bag. She had tried to break the door panels by sheer force, but their strength had defied her.

Now she wandered aimlessly about the dimly lighted circular room. Hungry and thirsty, she grew more and more desperate. What had become of George? And Bess? In utter dismay Nancy realized that she had the car keys with her.

She sank down on the bottom step of the winding iron staircase to try to figure things out. Staring straight ahead at the dusty wooden floor, she thought, "This is the worst trap I've ever been in!"

Suddenly she became aware of something in the floor. A tiny crack outlined a space about three feet square. Because of the gloom and dust, she had not noticed it before.

"Speaking of traps," Nancy muttered, "maybe this is a trap door!"

Quickly she dropped to her hands and knees and inspected the crack. Obviously it marked the outline of an opening, but there was no ring or handle with which to pull up the wood.

Nancy pried at first with her fingers, then with the nail file. The slender bit of steel snapped in her hands!

"Oh, how can I get this door open?" she thought, looking for something heavier.

There was not a single object in the tower room. After a while she sighed in despair. The room seemed to be growing stuffy. Or was it because she felt almost ill from hunger? Her tongue parched and her head aching, she slowly climbed the stairs and went out on the parapet for some fresh air.

The sky became overcast. In a short time it would be almost dark. Except for the occasional hoot of an owl and the intermittent croaking of frogs, there was no sound.

Then suddenly Nancy heard approaching footsteps. Her first impulse was to shout, but intuition warned her to remain silent.

Cautiously she looked over the parapet. A man was unlocking the door far below her! He snapped on a flashlight and entered the tower.

Nancy's heart pounded. Should she walk boldly down the stairs and try to bluff her way out?

"No," she decided. "I'm sure something sinister is going on at Heath Castle, and this man probably is involved. Maybe I can get out of here while he's busy. He may have opened that trap door and gone below."

Nancy tiptoed across the little balcony room. Suddenly a light flashed through the open doorway. The beam missed her by a fraction of an inch!

As she shrank into the shadows, Nancy heard the man coming up the iron staircase. With sinking heart, she stepped in back of the door and pressed herself against the wall.

The intruder went directly to the parapet. As Nancy peered out, he began to flash his light slowly as if he were signaling. The backward reflection of the rays dimly revealed his face. Nancy had never seen this cruel-looking man before.

Though the young detective longed to watch what he was doing, she dared not linger. Silently she slipped through the door and darted down the steps. Upon reaching the courtyard garden, she hurried to the arched doorway. Luckily it was still unlocked.

Nancy groped her way through the dark corridor in the castle. A moment later she bumped her knee into a piece of furniture and struck it so hard that she nearly cried out in pain.

Precious minutes were lost as she carefully felt

The intruder went directly to the parapet.

along walls for a door to the grounds. At last her efforts were rewarded. With a deep sigh of relief, she rushed into the open.

"What an adventure!" Nancy shuddered. "Now if only I can find George and Bess!"

Nancy made her way back to the tool house. It was empty. From there she walked toward the main gate, but because of weed-grown paths and treacherous rocks it took her quite a while before she saw the vague outline of a wall ahead of her.

"I hope it's close to the gate," she thought. "Oh—"

Something was moving through the bushes. In an instant the stillness was broken by the sharp barking of dogs.

"Can I make it?" Nancy wondered. She leaped for the wall and scrambled up just as the two hounds arrived. Breathlessly she dropped to the other side. Five minutes later she came to the car. To her amazement and delight George was huddled on the back seat. She was half asleep.

"George!"

The girl sat bolt upright. "Nancy!"

"I'm so sorry I left you," Nancy apologized, then asked, "Where's Bess?"

"Gone to get your father. What in the world happened to you?"

"Plenty. But first, tell me what time Bess left."

"It seems hours ago. It's a long walk to a bus

or a phone. Somebody should be here any minute, though."

As the girls sat in the car, they told each other their adventures.

"After Bess left," George concluded, "I heard a noise in the distance. I hid in the bushes near the gate. Mr. Hector drove out. While he was locking the gate, I peeked into his car to see if you were there. I really expected you to be lying on the floor, bound and gagged!"

"I was a prisoner, all right, but not tied up."

"I'd like to find the boy who took my clothes," George said grimly.

"Did you recognize him?"

"I never saw him before. He was about twelve years old. But I'd like to wring his neck."

"I spotted him from the tower," Nancy said. "He looked like Teddy Hooper, but I'm not sure."

George changed the subject. "Where do you suppose that man in the tower came from. No one besides Hector drove in here."

"He must have entered from the beach, the way the boy did," Nancy replied.

Headlights cut the darkness. Was it Carson Drew? Or was Daniel Hector returning?

The two girls ducked out of sight. The car stopped and Bess alighted.

"Why, George is gone!" she exclaimed.

"No, she isn't," her cousin spoke up, coming out of hiding.

Nancy was already running to the car from which her father had stepped. In an instant she was in his arms.

"Why, Dad, you're trembling!" she said.

"Nancy, Nancy, I'm so glad to see you. You gave me such a fright. Where—?"

"I'm sorry I made a mess of things," his daughter apologized. "But maybe you'll forgive me when you hear what happened."

"Tell me about it on the way back. Bess can drive George and herself home in your car. We'll follow them, and you can take the car the rest of the way."

On the drive to River Heights Mr. Drew listened to Nancy's story without comment. "I'm convinced," she concluded, "that a group is searching for something at Heath Castle. The walls there aren't crumbling from age. They're being tampered with!"

"I agree it looks mighty suspicious," Mr. Drew said. "And Daniel Hector seems to be involved. But suppose you put the whole case out of your mind until you've had a square meal."

Upon reaching home, Nancy went directly to the kitchen. Hannah Gruen, who had been nearly beside herself with worry, embraced the girl.

"You poor child!" she said. "I'll fix you a warm supper right away."

Hannah hastened to prepare the meal. Too hungry to wait, Nancy helped herself to a glass of milk and a few cookies. As she ate and drank, she related her adventure to the housekeeper.

"Oh, Nancy!" Mrs. Gruen sighed. "Your love of mystery will prove your undoing! You must be more careful."

Mr. Drew said, "I think you'd better stay away from Heath Castle."

"Oh, Dad!" she protested.

"Why not forget the whole affair for a few days?"

"But time is so short—"

"As it happens, I'm going away on a little trip, Nancy. I thought you might enjoy coming along."

Nancy shook her head. "If you'll excuse me, Dad, I believe I'd rather stay here and try to solve the mystery of Juliana."

"I'm sorry," Mr. Drew said, his eyes twinkling. "I thought Hampton might prove of interest to you, especially since it was the town where Juliana Johnson was advised to go."

Nancy could scarcely believe her ears. "Say that again, Dad!"

"I was talking with Dr. Gibson in Henryville today," Mr. Drew revealed. "I learned he was Juliana's physician. In fact, he told her to take the trip from which she never returned."

"Tell me more!"

"There's not much to tell. Juliana was thin

and run-down, so the doctor advised her to take a vacation. He suggested she slip off to a quiet place without letting anyone know where she was going."

"Did the doctor know where she went?"

"No, but he had suggested Hampton. At the time of her disappearance, the police tried to locate her there, but were unsuccessful."

"Oh, Dad, I give in," Nancy said excitedly. "I'll go with you!"

"I rather thought you would," Mr. Drew said with a smile.

"When do we leave?"

"Tomorrow morning. Better pack tonight!"

CHAPTER X

In Search of a Clue

WHEN Nancy appeared in the kitchen the next morning, Hannah Gruen said cheerily, "Good morning. There's a letter for you I think you'll want to see right away."

Nancy went to the hall table to get it. A glance at the handwriting caused her pulse to quicken. The letter was from Ned Nickerson!

Nancy eagerly opened the envelope. She missed her special friend who had gone to South America on a school project.

Ned wrote, "I'm doing some interesting work, but I miss you and the fun we had solving mysteries. I'll bet you're head over heels in one this very minute!"

"Right you are, Ned!" Nancy smiled happily as she tucked the letter away for another reading.

Mr. Drew came downstairs and said they should eat at once and then leave. Nancy suggested that they stop at Mrs. Fenimore's house. She wanted to ask a question about Juliana.

"All right," Mr. Drew agreed.

Mrs. Fenimore said she was happy to see Nancy again and pleased to meet her father.

"We're en route to Hampton," Mr. Drew explained. "I've given your sister's strange disappearance considerable thought. Apparently she abandoned her career very suddenly."

"Oh, Juliana loved her work!" Mrs. Fenimore protested. "Of course, she was tired, but a few weeks' rest should have restored her to good health."

Nancy remarked, "But after leaving here, Juliana never danced again—at least not under her own name. She may be doing some other kind of work. Did your sister have any special aptitudes for something besides dancing?"

Mrs. Fenimore shrugged. "She loved gardening."

There was nothing more the woman could tell the Drews, so Nancy and her father said good-by.

"You know," the lawyer commented as he led the way to the car, "Juliana may have married."

"But, Dad, she was engaged to Walter Heath!"

"True. Well, perhaps in Hampton we'll find a clue to her disappearance."

Mr. Drew got into the car. Nancy was about to follow when she observed a thin, sharp-faced woman with unkempt hair hanging clothes in the yard adjoining the Fenimore house.

"That must be Teddy Hooper's mother," she thought. Her attention was not centered on the woman, but on the clothes she was pinning to the line. A blue shirt looked familiar to Nancy.

"If that isn't George's stolen shirt, it's just like it!" she decided. On impulse she ran over to the yard. The woman saw her coming and eyed the girl suspiciously.

"Is Teddy here?" Nancy inquired.

"No. He's at school, same as every day."

Nancy asked Mrs. Hooper if Teddy liked to go boating on the river.

"All boys play around the water," the woman answered. Then she added quickly, "He ain't been on the river lately, though."

Nancy was convinced Mrs. Hooper was not telling the truth. "That's a lovely shirt," she went on.

"Ain't I got a right to have nice things, like other folks?" the woman demanded defiantly.

"Why, certainly," Nancy said evenly. But she was still sure the shirt belonged to George.

"You must be another one of those snoopy policewomen!" Teddy's mother snapped. "Well, I won't talk to you!" She snatched the shirt from the line and hurried into the house.

Nancy returned to the car and related the conversation to her father. "I must talk to Teddy when we get back," she added.

The Drews started for Hampton. An unexpected detour extended the trip by many miles, and a lunch with slow service delayed them. They did not arrive until two-thirty at the Hampton Motel.

"Meet me here at six, Nancy," the lawyer said and drove off.

The young detective decided there was no use going to the usual places to make inquiries about Juliana, since the police had investigated them years ago.

"If Juliana wanted to live here incognito, where would she go?" Nancy asked herself. She felt that inconspicuous tourist homes might be the answer.

She hurried to the Chamber of Commerce and obtained a list of guesthouses. With the photograph of Juliana for identification of the dancer, she walked from one house to another. Some of the owners recognized the woman in the picture, but none had rented a room to her. Finally Nancy rang the doorbell of the last place on her list. After a few minutes a small, gray-haired woman appeared.

"If you're looking for a room, I'm afraid I'll have to disappoint you," she said before Nancy could speak. "I don't take guests any more."

"I don't want a room," Nancy replied with a

smile. "I came to ask about someone who might have stayed with you at some time." She showed the photograph.

"Come in," the woman said cordially. "I think I can help you!"

Nancy's heart leaped. Could it be true?

"I'm Mrs. Delbert," the woman said as she led her caller into a neat, old-fashioned living room. "You are—?"

"Nancy Drew. I'm a stranger in Hampton. What name did your guest give you?"

"Let me think. I remember now. She was Miss Flower. Julia Flower. Is she a friend of yours?"

"Mrs. Delbert, if she really was the person in this picture, she was a famous dancer who disappeared ten years ago. I know her sister."

It was Mrs. Delbert's turn to look shocked. "My, my!" she said. "How dreadful! It was ten years ago that she was here."

"Just one more question: Did Miss Flower say where she was going after she left here?"

"Yes, she spoke of staying on a farm between Hopewell and Plainville, but she didn't tell me the name of the people."

"Is it far from here?" Nancy asked.

"About thirty miles. Miss Flower said she'd take the bus and walk into the farm from the main road. All she had was a purse and a small suitcase."

"You have a terrific memory," Nancy said.

Mrs. Delbert smiled. "Julia Flower was the most beautiful guest I ever had!"

Nancy got up and put an arm around the woman. "Thank you so much," she said. "You've been a great help." After saying good-by, Nancy hurried back to the motel and told her father what she had learned.

"You've done well, Nancy, and picked up an excellent clue. You should have a reward for that good bit of detecting."

Nancy grinned. "As a reward, will you take me to Plainville when you finish your work here?"

"Yes, indeed. I'll be through by noon tomorrow."

The Drews checked out at twelve o'clock the next day and drove toward Plainville. When they came to Hopewell, Nancy suggested they inquire at police headquarters about the missing dancer.

She spoke to a middle-aged sergeant and showed him Juliana's picture. He looked at it thoughtfully and finally said:

"I don't know that this will help you, but about ten years ago another officer and I were called on an accident case. A young woman had been struck by a car on a side road and was found unconscious and badly bruised. Hit-and-run driver and no witnesses. She was taken to a hospital in Plainville. No identification or purse or luggage."

"Probably stolen," Mr. Drew commented.

"She looked a little like the person in this

photograph," the officer went on. "A funny thing about the case was, when nurses undressed her at the hospital, they found several thousands of dollars on her."

"Did the police find out why?" Nancy asked.

"No. She insisted she had drawn it from her savings account because she was traveling. Why don't you stop at the hospital? Maybe they can answer your questions."

Nancy said she was grateful for this good lead. She returned to the car and told her father. They set off at once for the hospital.

The superintendent received them courteously. After hearing their story, she showed them some old records. No one by the name of Juliana or Julie Johnson had been a patient at the institution, but a Julia Flower had been!

Only the word "traveler" had been written in the space for the home address.

The superintendent anticipated Nancy's next question. "Where did she go after she was released from here? I don't know."

Seeing the girl's disappointment, she said, "You might talk to Joe. He's been our maintenance man for twenty years. A friendly fellow. And his memory for patients is amazing."

While Mr. Drew waited in the lobby, Nancy went to the basement to find Joe. When she showed him the photograph, a wide grin spread over his face.

"Indeed I remember that girl. She called her-self Julia Flower. I felt sorry for her when she left here in a wheelchair. She was crying her eyes out as the nurse rolled her to the elevator."

"Why was she crying?" Nancy asked.

"I overheard Dr. Barnes tell Miss Flower she'd never be able to walk properly again."

"Is Dr. Barnes still with the hospital?"

"No. He went to New York to head up a large clinic."

"How about nurses who took care of her?" Nancy inquired.

"I remember one. She was nice—Miss Emily Foster. I don't know what became of her."

"Do you have any idea where Miss Flower went?"

Joe shook his head. "She didn't say."

The man's information threw new light on the mystery. Nancy thanked him and hurried back to her father.

"Such an injury could have prevented Juliana from ever dancing again," she said.

Mr. Drew nodded. "The thought of her admir-ers feeling pity for her may have been too much for Juliana to bear. Perhaps she dropped out of sight on purpose!"

"She probably took an assumed name in order to avoid publicity, then disappeared because she didn't want to be a burden to her sister," Nancy said. "Juliana's pride kept her from marrying Walter Heath." Nancy paused a moment. "Oh, Dad, we're really getting somewhere!"

At the main desk Nancy and her father tried to obtain the doctor's and the nurse's address.

"Dr. Barnes died three years ago," the receptionist said. "As for Emily Foster, I have an old address, but I understand she left the place some time ago. However, the people who live there might be able to tell you where she is."

While Mr. Drew registered at the local motel for his daughter and himself, Nancy hurried on foot to the designated address. To her disappointment she found the residence occupied by new tenants who had never heard of Emily Foster.

"Another blind alley!" Nancy sighed as she started back to join her father.

As she walked along the street Nancy became aware of a man walking a little distance behind her. At first she thought nothing of it, but after three blocks she concluded someone must be following her.

Nancy quickened her pace. After six blocks, she still had not shaken the person and decided to get a good look at him. She dropped her handbag on purpose. As she turned to pick it up, Nancy gazed directly at the man. He wore a brown suit and had a sharp, angular face and dark eyes.

When he realized that Nancy knew she was being followed, he wheeled around and turned down a side street.

"He *was* tailing me!" Nancy thought.

She had never seen the man before and wondered why he was trailing her. She was eager to tell her father, but found that he had invited a client to dinner. By ten o'clock, after the caller had gone, she had stopped thinking about the incident.

Before retiring, father and daughter sat down in Mr. Drew's bedroom to discuss the mystery.

"Isn't Emily Foster our best lead yet?" Nancy asked.

Mr. Drew did not answer; in fact, for several seconds he had not been paying strict attention to Nancy's conversation. Now, so suddenly that the young detective was startled, he tiptoed to the door and yanked it open.

A man in a brown suit crouched just outside. Thrown off balance, he fell forward into the room.

CHAPTER XI

A Warning

"So you were eavesdropping!" Mr. Drew said sternly as he pulled the man to his feet.

"No, that's not true!" the fellow stammered. After recovering his balance, he tried to retreat.

Mr. Drew blocked the doorway. "Sit down!" he ordered the man into the room. "We want to talk to you."

Nancy recognized the man as the one who had followed her.

"What were you doing outside my door?" Mr. Drew asked him sharply.

"Nothing," he replied in a sullen voice. "I thought this room belonged to a friend."

"That's hard to believe, but easy enough to check. What's his name?"

"None of your business."

"I can turn you over to the police."

Nancy spoke up. "I can report to them that you trailed me today!"

The stranger squirmed uneasily in the chair. "You can't prove anything!"

"This man followed you today?" Mr. Drew asked his daughter in surprise.

"Yes. I forgot to tell you about it."

"That settles it," the lawyer said. "We'll turn him over to the police for questioning."

"No, no! Don't do that! I'll tell anything you want to know—except my name," the stranger said.

"Very well." The lawyer nodded. "Why were you following my daughter?"

"Because I was paid to do it."

"By whom?"

"I don't know the guy's name."

"What were your instructions?"

"To make a complete report on where Miss Drew went, whom she talked to, and what she did."

Mr. Drew turned so that the man could not see him full face. With a wink and a quick movement of his hand he signaled Nancy to step into the adjoining room. For a moment the young detective was puzzled. Then it dawned upon her that her father wanted her to slip quietly downstairs and arrange to have the stranger followed.

"So you won't tell us your name?" Mr. Drew repeated, facing the stranger once more and walking up so close to him the man could not see Nancy.

"No. I won't," the man replied.

Nancy stole noiselessly into the adjoining room. She hastened downstairs and used a public telephone to call police headquarters. After identifying her father and herself, she said, "Please send a plainclothesman at once. I'll meet him in the lobby and explain everything when he arrives. How will I know him?"

"He'll pretend to have a bad cold," the officer said.

Nancy was worried that the detective might not reach the hotel in time. But in less than five minutes a man entered coughing uncontrollably. She told him why he had been called and asked him to trail the eavesdropper.

"Here he comes now!" she whispered as the brown-suited stranger emerged from an elevator. "He must not see me!"

She hid behind a pillar and noticed with satisfaction that the eavesdropper did not realize he was being followed from the hotel. Then she went upstairs.

Mr. Drew praised his daughter for having interpreted his signals correctly. "By the way," he asked, "have you called Hannah since we left home? There may be some messages for us."

At once Nancy dialed the Drew number. Hannah Gruen answered.

"I'm glad you phoned," she said. "I tried to reach you in Hampton, but you had already left."

"Is anything wrong?"

"Mrs. Fenimore called this morning and wanted to see you."

"Mrs. Fenimore?" Nancy echoed in curiosity. "Did she say why she called?"

"She wouldn't tell me over the phone," Hannah resumed. "When I told her you weren't home, she said you had to be warned to be careful."

"Careful of what?"

"She thinks you're in danger. Oh, Nancy, I'll be so relieved when you're home again safe and unharmed."

"We'll be back tomorrow," Nancy assured her. "Don't worry."

After completing the call Nancy speculated on why Mrs. Fenimore thought the young detective was in danger. Could the woman have learned that Nancy was to be shadowed? It was too late, she decided, to call Mrs. Fenimore. "I'll see her tomorrow."

Nancy and her father waited until midnight to hear from the plainclothesman. When he failed to return to the hotel, they telephoned headquarters. The officer had not checked in yet.

In the morning there was no word either, so Mr. Drew requested that a full report be sent to him in River Heights.

After Nancy arrived home in the afternoon, she lost no time calling on Mrs. Fenimore. The woman was reclining on a couch. She was exhausted from strain and worry.

"I shouldn't have become so upset," she said. "But Mr. Hector's attitude always disturbs me."

"He came to see you?"

"Yes. I had a dreadful session with him. He asked me so many questions."

"About your sister?"

The woman nodded. "He wanted to know if I had hired someone to search for Julie."

"Did you mention my name?"

"Well, I did say you had offered to help me," Mrs. Fenimore admitted, "though I feel unhappy about having told him. From the way he behaved, I'm sure he intends to make trouble for you."

"I'm not afraid of Daniel Hector," Nancy said.

"Oh, but you should have heard him talk! He said he wouldn't let anyone meddle in his affairs. He acted as if Heath Castle belongs to him!"

"Mr. Hector is worried," Nancy commented, frowning. "His remarks and the fact that he came to talk to you regarding your sister indicate a guilty conscience."

"Would you risk going to Heath Castle again, Nancy?"

"I would if I could accomplish something," the young detective said. "But I believe the mystery may be solved in another way."

She thought it best not to tell Mrs. Fenimore about the possibility that her sister might have

been crippled as a result of an automobile accident. She merely said there was an interesting
new lead to follow, one which would not involve
her coming in contact with Daniel Hector.

Later, at home, Nancy reviewed the developments in the mystery. Intruders prowling around
the Heath estate were looking for something important. She had heard them mention the clue in
a stone wall and unnamed items they had already
found. Where did Hector fit in? Were they all
working together? What—if anything—did the
search have to do with Juliana's disappearance?

"And then there's the man who was eavesdropping," Nancy thought as she opened the top
drawer of her dresser to get a handkerchief. There
lay the torn note she had found in the debris at
the Heath factory. In the recent excitement she
had forgotten about it.

"This may be my most valuable clue," she
chided herself. "I must try to figure it out."

She sat down to piece out the message. Just
then the telephone rang. The caller was George
who wanted to know how the detective work was
progressing.

"I have a clue to your stolen clothes," Nancy
said, and told of the shirt at Mrs. Hooper's.

"Why, the nerve of that woman!" George cried
indignantly. "I'm going there at once and demand
that she return my property!"

"You can't prove anything, George," Nancy said. "Better forget the matter for the time being, and come over here. I have lots to tell you. Bring Bess along."

"Be there pronto," George replied and hung up.

"If it was really Teddy who took those clothes," Nancy reasoned, "what was *he* doing in the Heath gardens?" She was still trying to figure this out when her friends arrived. Nancy told them everything that had happened on her trip.

"Poor Juliana!" Bess said. "How dreadful to have her career cut off that way!"

"I wish you could have found the nurse Emily Foster," George added. "Well, what are you going to work on next?"

"This note, or rather, this piece of a note."

Nancy produced the bit of paper and the girls pored over it for some time, each with a pencil and paper, trying to fill in the lines to form a logical message. Bess was the first one to claim having pieced together the missing words.

"Listen to this," she said. "I've got it!

" 'Dear C,
       Some place is the se-
cret which I hid
in a wall. I want to be
famous. If I can sell it, I will be
worthy of you.' "

George scoffed. "If he was going to sell it, why would he hide it in a wall?"

"Well, it fits the missing words," Bess defended herself.

"One guess is as good as another," Nancy said, then she stared thoughtfully at the paper before her. Suddenly she jumped up from the chair and said, "The solution to this mystery might be right in this very house!"

Without explaining her strange remark, Nancy ran from her room and down the stairs. A few minutes later she returned with a large book.

"How in the world are you going to find Juliana with that?" George asked.

The book contained a collection of colored photographs and descriptions of famous old homes and gardens in England.

"I forgot I had this," Nancy said, quickly turning the pages. "Look here!"

"Heath Castle!" exclaimed George.

"The original one in England. Only it wasn't called Heath, of course."

"And the gardens," cried Bess as they scanned picture after picture. Nancy was reading a description under one of them when suddenly a paragraph below caught her eyes.

"Listen to this! I think we have the clue we've been looking for!"

CHAPTER XII

Secret Entrance

GEORGE and Bess studied the paragraph to which Nancy had pointed. It had been written in Middle English. Nancy had learned in school to read the works of the poet Chaucer, who wrote in that language. Eagerly she translated the quotation.

" 'I have hidden my treasures in the niches of the cloister through which, all unsuspecting, the noble men and fair ladies pass each day to bathe.' "

"Sounds quaint," Bess said. "But how does it help us?"

"Don't you see?" Nancy said. "Ira Heath built his estate to resemble the one in England. Probably he and his son knew about the old cloister."

"Granted." George nodded. "But so what?"

"If the Heaths had a treasure to hide, wouldn't *their* cloister have been a good place to put it?"

"Do you really think they had a treasure?" Bess asked.

"I don't know," Nancy replied, "but I have a hunch they did. We know certain men are searching for a clue, but they also mentioned having found other things. Perhaps those were part of the treasure."

"Is there a cloister in the Heath gardens?" George asked. "I haven't seen one."

Nancy turned the page. The three girls looked at the picture on it, which showed a long passageway flanked by columns leading toward a river.

"This is the cloister!" said Nancy excitedly. "Oh, I wonder whether there's one at Heath Castle!"

"You didn't notice it from the tower?" Bess inquired.

"N-no," Nancy answered slowly. "But there was something leading from the castle toward the river—a kind of tunnel covered with vines."

"I'll bet that's it," George said enthusiastically. "Listen! The bell. Someone's at the door."

Nancy went downstairs to see who it was. The caller proved to be Salty.

"And how are ye, lass?" he asked with a smile. "Sorry I can't give ye any report about that fellow what crashed into ye. I been lookin' high an' low for his boat, but I ain't seen any part o' her."

"Thank you. You've been very helpful," Nancy

said, then added, "Salty, I'm thinking of going to the Heath gardens by boat. Have you ever noticed a—a sort of tunnel there, leading from the beach?"

"Can't say I have," the clam digger replied. "Are you figurin' on lookin' for one?"

Nancy smiled as she said, "Perhaps some time when you're not busy—"

Salty suddenly slapped his thigh and chuckled. "Women!" he said. "They never come right out an' say what they want. Nancy, I'll meet you an' your friends at Campbell's Landing ten o'clock sharp tomorrow mornin', barrin' rain."

Nancy thanked him. "Another thing, Salty. I'd like to find out about Walter Heath's experiments. Are you sure you can't tell me more about them?"

The man shook his head. "I don't know a thing more. But maybe Sam Weatherby can help ye."

"The curio dealer?"

"Sam worked at the Heath factory before he went into business for himself. He knew Walt as well as anyone in town."

"Then I'll go to see Sam Weatherby!" Nancy said, grateful for the information.

Soon after Salty had gone down the street, Bess and George left for home, promising to be on hand the next morning. Nancy drove to Sam Weatherby's shop.

"Haven't seen you in a while," he greeted her cheerfully. "Did you bring that pearl and the shell I offered to buy?"

Nancy told him the pearl had been stolen.

"That's too bad," the man said sympathetically. "Well, maybe you'll find a bigger one."

"I hope so," Nancy said with a smile. "But right now I'm more interested in Walter Heath's experiments."

She told about the pile of crushed and broken whelk shells she had found at the pond. "The colors were so beautiful, I've been wondering if he was trying to make dye from them."

"You guessed right," Mr. Weatherby said, eyeing her intently. "So far as I know, Walt had no luck, but he kept working at it. And once he said to me, 'Sam, even if I don't succeed in making a fortune in dye, there's another treasure on my estate.' Then he winked and said, 'It's right in plain sight, too!' "

"What did he mean by that?" Nancy asked.

The dealer shrugged. "Who knows? Walt was like that—full of riddles and secrets. In one way his experimental work brought him luck."

"How?"

"He found a big pearl; at least, that's what he told me. Said he was going to present it to a young lady friend of his—a dancer."

Nancy blinked in astonishment at the revelation. Had he really given the pearl to Juliana?

Or was it hidden in one of the cloister walls? And was that what someone was looking for?

Nancy thanked the curio dealer for his information and turned to leave. An object in the showcase caught her eye. Lying in a velvet-lined case was the antique charm from a man's watch chain that Daniel Hector had sold to Mr. Weatherby.

"Handsome, isn't it?" the jeweler remarked, taking the charm from its case. "An old English family design. A genuine heirloom."

Nancy admired the piece of jewelry. Mr. Weatherby also showed her a pair of earrings, a bracelet, and a brooch, all bearing the same design.

"Daniel Hector sold me this entire set," Mr. Weatherby revealed. "That lawyer is a hard customer, though. He argues for the last penny."

"Did he inherit these from English ancestors?" Nancy asked.

"That's what he said. Between you and me, I think he got them from a client who couldn't pay a bill."

Nancy wondered if Hector had received the charm and the other pieces of jewelry honestly, but kept quiet.

When Nancy reached home she learned that during her absence a call had come from Hopewell. Either she or her father was to get in touch with the man who had phoned.

"He was a detective," Hannah Gruen told her, "and he wouldn't give me a message."

Nancy called headquarters at Hopewell. The plainclothesman was out at the time but had left his report for her. The stranger he had shadowed the night before had driven to River Heights. From there he had gone to the abandoned Heath factory to meet another man.

"If I only knew who that person was!" Nancy exclaimed.

"I have a description of him," said the police sergeant and read it. Nancy was almost certain he was the same man who had damaged her motorboat! She thanked the officer, then hung up. The young detective mulled over what she had just heard.

Obviously the intruders at Heath Castle knew she was working on the case and had sent someone to shadow her. Would they stop there? Or was she in danger? Her father was out of town on business, so she could not discuss the matter with him. Finally she went to bed.

The next morning Nancy put the key to the front door of Heath Castle in a pocket of her slacks, then hastened to Campbell's Landing. She was the first to arrive and arranged to rent a motorboat. She was just getting it ready when George and Bess arrived. Finally Salty showed up in his rowboat, which he fastened securely to the larger craft, then jumped in with the girls.

"All set!" he announced. "Cast off!"

The girls enjoyed the ride upstream; not only because it was beautiful on the river, but because the clam digger entertained them with songs and stories of the sea.

Soon the girls saw the high turrets of Heath Castle in the distance. Nancy recalled the man she had seen signaling from one of them with a flashlight.

"His helper was probably waiting on the water," she thought.

The shoreline was matted thickly with bushes, and only a narrow beach was visible. Above it stood a high, weather-stained wall, the river barrier of Heath Castle.

"Let's anchor the motorboat in the river and take the little one ashore," Salty suggested.

They untied the rowboat and climbed aboard. With powerful strokes the sailor sent it surging through the water. Presently it grounded on the shore and they stepped out.

The girls left Salty, who wanted to look for clams along the beach. The young sleuths turned their attention to the high wall which marked the rear boundary of the Heath estate. Only the treetops above the gardens were visible. Directly in front of the wall grew tall brier bushes.

Nancy and her friends walked along the beach. "That boy who stole your clothes seemed to appear out of nowhere," Nancy said. "I didn't see him scale a wall. He must have reached the beach some other way."

"You mean by the cloister?" asked Bess.

"Maybe. I'm sure there's an opening along here."

Pushing ahead, she began to examine the base. Finally, parting some brier bushes, she saw several large stones which apparently never had been cemented into the wall. She pushed against the center one. It moved easily!

"Girls, this may be an entrance!" Nancy cried out.

CHAPTER XIII

Treasure!

NANCY pressed against the center stone in the wall. It moved inward to reveal a flight of eight steps leading upward to an arched passageway.

"The cloister!" Bess and George exclaimed.

One side of the passageway was set with square stone columns. Heavy vines grew up and over them, forming a roof of leaves through which sunlight filtered into the cool tunnel. The other side was a high crumbling fieldstone wall with deep alcoves about twenty-five feet apart.

"Just like the picture we saw in the book!" Bess said. "Oh, what an attractive walk to the beach!"

"Now to find the hidden treasure," George said. "Come on!"

Hopefully the girls examined the niches along the wall, some of which had built-in stone shelves. In one, a statuette lay on its side; in another, a vase had tipped over and broken.

George felt among the vines. "Nothing here—" she started to say when Nancy interrupted her. She held up a finger in warning.

"Listen!" she whispered.

The three girls stood still. Faintly they heard men's voices from the other side of the wall. They stole along the flagstones cautiously, hardly daring to breathe. As they reached another niche, the deep voices came to them distinctly.

"This looks like a good spot!" one man said, making no attempt to speak low. "Bring your pick, Cobb."

Nancy recognized the voices. *She had heard them the night of her imprisonment in the tower!*

The men started to work with chisel, pick, and sledgehammer. Tiny stones and bits of mortar rattled down at the girls' feet.

"They're wrecking this lovely wall!" George whispered indignantly.

Just then a decorative ledge in the alcove came loose and threatened to crash to the flagstone floor. Quickly Nancy stepped forward and caught the slab. With Bess's help, she laid it carefully on the ground.

Nancy straightened up and gasped as she looked at the wall niche. Where the ledge had been, a long, narrow pocket was now exposed!

Nancy ran her hand into the dark opening. Her groping fingers touched something cold and hard.

A metal box!

"Nancy!" George warned in a whisper.

Directly above the girl's hand a stone chisel was poking through the wall. In another moment the men would succeed in making a large opening into the niche!

Nancy drew out the flat metal box, then the three girls turned and fled through the cloister toward the castle. The sound of the men working gradually died away.

"We're safe!" Nancy exclaimed. "Now let's open the box!"

Her hands trembled with excitement as she lifted the lid of the rusty container.

"Hm!" said George. "Only papers and photographs."

Bess, too, was disappointed. "There's nothing valuable here! And after all our trouble, too!"

"Let's not be too hasty," Nancy advised, and lifted out the top photograph carefully. Yellowed with age, it showed a middle-aged man in old-fashioned clothes. At the bottom was scrawled the name "Ira Heath," and a date.

Nancy was about to hand the picture to George when a detail of the man's clothing attracted her attention. A watch chain which hung from Mr. Heath's vest pocket had an unusual charm attached to it!

"Look at this!" she said. "I saw the very same charm at Sam Weatherby's curio shop. Daniel

Hector sold it to him along with some other jewelry!"

"You're kidding!" Bess exclaimed.

"No. Hector told Mr. Weatherby the jewelry was from his own family."

"That certainly sounds suspicious," George said, reaching for another photograph. She held up the picture of a sweet-faced woman, wearing a long gown and upswept hair. An inscription identified her as Heath's wife, Ida.

"Her earrings!" Nancy said. "Hector sold those to Mr. Weatherby, too!"

"He has been robbing the estate!" Bess declared.

There were more pictures in the box, but none were of particular interest to the girls. Underneath the pile was a small leather-bound diary. The flyleaf bore Walter Heath's name, and the dates of many of the notations showed they had been made less than a month before his death.

"This may be the most valuable thing in this box!" Nancy remarked, skimming through the book. Many of the pages were blank, but under one date was an item important enough to read aloud.

" 'I stumbled upon something which may prove to be a treasure. In the salted pond there are many marine mollusks placed there by my father. They not only have beautiful shells, but their glands give off a purple dye. I am mixing it with

" 'I stumbled upon something which may prove to be a treasure!' " Nancy read aloud.

certain chemicals and so far have produced six shades of purple dye. But the color does not last. I will keep trying for a perfect formula."

"I wonder if he did perfect it and what became of the formula," Bess mused.

"Good question," said George.

Nancy turned more pages in the diary. "Here's something," she said. "Listen to this:

" 'I don't trust the new chauffeur Biggs. Have decided to hide all the bottles of dye until my experiments are complete.' "

"Does it say where he hid them?" George asked. "Read the next page."

"There's nothing more. This is the last paragraph in the book."

"What a shame!"

"Maybe we'll find other clues when we read the entire diary," Nancy said. "But there's no time now."

"I'll say there isn't!" George agreed. *"Sh!* We'd better duck out of here and fast!"

From just across the stone barrier came the barking of a dog. Voices were audible, and each moment they grew louder. The two men were approaching!

"How about looking on the opposite side of this wall?" one of them asked.

"Okay," the other man replied. "May as well climb over and make a good job of it while we're here."

Fearful of being seen, the girls tiptoed along the cloister wall. Nancy carried the metal box, which was heavy.

"We should have gone the other way, toward the beach," she whispered. "I hope we don't get trapped!"

As they rounded a curve the girls noticed that the cloister ended abruptly in a rear wall of the castle, with a huge wooden door. It was locked! Nancy tried her key. It would not fit!

"Oh, what'll we do?" Bess asked. "This is awful!"

The men could be heard moving slowly up the flagstone passageway. In a moment or two they certainly would see the girls.

"Nancy, we'll have to hide the box!" George said.

"We'd better hide ourselves," Bess urged.

"Maybe we could break through the vines," Nancy suggested.

"No chance," George decided. "There's a network of thick stalks between the pillars. I touched them before when we were searching for the treasure."

Not far from the castle wall was a large nook. In their haste the girls had passed it with only a fleeting glance. Now Nancy thought that it might make a safe hiding place.

"Follow me!" she directed.

Above the arched entrance to the refuge had

been chiseled the words *Poet's Nook,* but the girls scarcely noticed it as they slipped into the niche.

"I must hide this box so the men can't take it, even if they catch us," Nancy declared grimly.

Frantically the girls looked about them. Nancy noticed a loose stone in the wall directly above a bench in the back of their hiding place.

"George," she said, "see if it will move."

Luckily the stone could be eased out. A large, empty space was behind it. Nancy slipped the box inside, and George quickly fitted the stone into place.

By this time the men were very near, and had stopped walking. "How about working in the Poet's Nook?" one asked suddenly. "Maybe we'll find something there."

The girls flattened themselves against the wall and waited tensely, scarcely daring to breathe.

"We looked there once. That hiding place over the bench was empty."

"Sure, but if we take out the whole wall, we might find another one. You're lazy if you ask me."

"Did I ask you?" the first man growled. "This is hard work. We're not getting much money for it either."

The other laughed. "What we found already is good enough pay for me. And if we find the other loot, we can live anyway we please."

Nancy and her friends surmised that the men

would not search the Poet's Nook again and relaxed slightly. But their hopes were dashed.

"How about it, Cobb?" the first man demanded. "Do we take out the wall or don't we?"

"Okay," the one addressed as Cobb replied. "You go ahead. I'll be with you in a minute. Here's the sledgehammer."

CHAPTER XIV

Cinderella's Slipper

NANCY, Bess, and George retreated deeper into the shadows, but their hearts sank. The men were sure to find them!

"I'll be right there, Biggs," Cobb called. "Just want to see if there's anything hidden in any of these other niches."

Biggs! The name electrified the girls. Hadn't Walter Heath mentioned the name Biggs in the diary as that of a suspicious person? Could he be the chauffeur, searching, perhaps, for the bottles of dye his former employer had hidden?

The next moment a tall figure appeared in the entrance of the niche with a sledgehammer. His back was turned to the girls as he called out:

"Hurry up! I'm not going to do the heavy work alone!"

At that instant the sound of running footsteps

could be heard. Startled, the speaker moved off in their direction.

Nancy tiptoed forward and peered out. Biggs was the man who had signaled from the tower! Then she saw a boy who was racing toward the two men. Teddy Hooper!

"Hey, come quick!" he shouted. "I've got something to show you!"

Cobb was irritated. "You again!" he exclaimed. "We told you to keep away from here!"

"But I've got something to tell you!"

"What is it?"

"First you pay me," the boy replied.

"Get out of here and leave us alone!"

"Maybe we'd better hear what Teddy has to say," Biggs urged. "It may be important."

"Gimme a dollar and I'll tell you," the boy demanded impudently.

"There!" Cobb snapped, handing over the money. "Now talk!"

"You know where the hole is in the beach wall? Somebody came through it."

"How do you know?"

"Footprints. Want to see 'em?"

"Okay." Cobb sounded concerned. "If anyone is on these premises, we'd better find out about it."

"Maybe the place is being watched! I'm clearing out of here!" Biggs added.

"Don't be a fool!" Cobb replied. "If anyone

came into the gardens through this passageway, he's got to go out the same way. All we have to do is watch the hole and we'll catch him."

The two men followed Teddy around the curve. When their voices died away, Nancy and the girls stepped from their hiding place.

"The boy was Teddy Hooper," Nancy said thoughtfully. "I wonder how he got mixed up with these men."

"Never mind him now," Bess said anxiously. "We must get out of here somehow, and fast!"

"As long as the men stay on the beach, we're pretty safe," Nancy replied. "But I'm worried about Salty. If only we had some way to warn him!"

"But how can we?" Bess asked. "Those men might pounce on us if we try to go."

"There's one possibility," George announced, pointing to a stone stairway between two of the columns which were intertwined with vines. "See if there's a way out through these."

The girls managed to force two of the heavy vines apart. Below them lay a small tangled garden.

"We can squeeze through here," Bess said. "Come on!"

"You go ahead," Nancy said. "I'll get the metal box."

A few minutes later she wriggled between the vines to join her friends. Eagerly they explored the little garden. It had sheer walls on three sides, too high to climb. They could not find a single opening!

Bess sat down in the middle of a weed-grown path. "I'm so discouraged I could cry," she admitted.

"Maybe a drink of water will revive you," her cousin suggested practically.

On the rear wall of the garden hung an artistic fountain from which spouted a little stream. Bess walked over to it and drank freely. "It's wonderful water," she said. "And cold. Must come from a spring."

Nancy and George cupped their hands and filled them several times. "It certainly tastes different from River Heights water," Nancy declared. "And you're right, it's delicious."

She was about to drink more when she spotted something on the crumbling wall just beneath the fountain. Parting the vines to get a better view, Nancy stared in astonishment.

"Girls, look! On the wall!" she exclaimed.

The vines had grown over a small block of cement which had been set into the stones. In it was the imprint of a woman's shoe. Beneath had been chiseled a single word: *Cinderella.*

"Cinderella's dancing slipper." George laughed. "Whoever would do such a crazy thing?"

"I'm not sure it was crazy," Nancy replied. "It's rather romantic and may have been Walter

Heath's way of paying a compliment to Juliana. Don't you recall that note I found in his handwriting which began 'Dear C'?"

"C could stand for a dozen other names," George said.

Nancy measured the dainty little shoe print with her hand. "But if it's Juliana's, it could be the clue Walter Heath mentioned in his will! He said she would be able to identify herself in a special way, and this could be it, couldn't it?"

"The print *is* very small," Bess admitted. "Not many girls wear such a tiny size."

"If we've really stumbled upon a secret, Nancy, we mustn't breathe a word of it!" Bess warned.

The other girls agreed and carefully covered the imprint with the vines.

"I wonder if there's anything of value hidden behind the cement block," Nancy mused.

"We can't find out today," George said. "We'd have to use tools to move it."

"It would be just our luck if Cobb and Biggs decide to smash the fountains," Nancy said. "Then we'd be too late." Suddenly she stiffened. "I hear someone!"

The girls became aware of a loud creaking noise from the cloister. "The rear castle door," whispered George.

Instantly they thought of the vines they had torn apart to get into the garden. Whoever was going in or out of the castle might notice the opening and come to investigate!

"Quick!" Nancy directed. "Lie down here in the tall grass and weeds!"

Bess and George flattened themselves on the ground. Nancy darted behind a bush leafy enough to hide her but not too thick to block her view.

A man, slightly stooped, came through the parted vines. He paused to examine them.

Nancy's heart stood still. He was Daniel Hector!

The lawyer peered into the garden, but evidently saw nothing unusual, because he went on toward the beach.

"Let's go!" Nancy whispered jubilantly a moment later. "The cloister entrance to the castle may have been left unlocked!"

The three girls stole noiselessly along and eventually reached the castle. The door was indeed unlocked. It made such a loud noise when Nancy pulled it that she feared the sound would carry to the men.

"What a weird place!" George commented as they hurried inside. Nancy led the way through the long winding corridor toward the front hall.

"Let's get out of here as soon as we can," Bess urged.

Nancy was fairly familiar with the floor plan and found the main entrance. It was locked, but the key she had fitted.

"At least we can get out," she said.

"No, no," Bess interrupted. "Hector probably has a guard on watch."

Not paying heed to her cousin's warning, George peeked outside, then stopped short. "Oh, oh!"

"What's the matter?" Bess asked, following her.

Tied at the foot of the steps were the two huge dogs the girls had met before. They began to growl menacingly.

"Well, hello, old fellows, we meet again!" Nancy called cheerily.

But her friendly attitude did not work this time. The animals would not allow the girls to descend.

"You try it alone, Nancy," Bess suggested.

Nancy had no success. "The hounds are acting very strangely," she whispered. "What can be wrong? The other day they let me pass." She shifted the metal box under her arm and the animals growled even more fiercely.

"Why, maybe it's this box," she said. "The dogs think I'm trying to steal something from the castle!"

Telling her friends she would be right back, Nancy ran inside. In a minute she had emptied the box of photographs and the diary and stuffed them under her sweater.

"Now where can I hide the box?" she thought.

Nancy caught sight of a narrow door, partially open. "That'll do," she decided.

As she placed the metal container on the floor of the closet, she heard footsteps not far away. Someone was coming along the winding corridor!

She hurried outside. The dogs growled but Nancy was determined to pass by them.

She ran down the steps, her friends behind her. Bess was fearful, but tried not to show it.

The hounds bayed loudly and the next second Mr. Hector's figure framed the doorway.

"Hey, you!" the lawyer shouted furiously. "Stop! Stop!"

The girls ignored him. As Hector ran down the steps to untie the dogs, he tripped over the long rope and fell down on his face.

Nancy urged her friends to run faster while the man bellowed in pain.

"Quick! To the wall!" she panted, holding the treasure close inside her sweater.

CHAPTER XV

Salty's Plight

THE three girls raced madly to the front wall of the estate. Clutching vines to pull themselves up, they reached the top and scrambled over. Then they paused for breath.

"What a narrow escape!" Nancy murmured. "Daniel Hector saw me!"

"Did he recognize you?" Bess asked.

"We have never really been introduced and I only turned around briefly when I first realized he was there."

"What did you do with the metal box?" Bess queried.

"I hid it. But not these." Nancy produced the photographs and the diary from beneath her sweater. "I still have the evidence!"

"Great!" George said. "But what's next? We're a long way from the boat."

After catching their breath, the girls debated what to do. They were worried about Salty and what might have happened to him. To reach him they would have to go far out of their way through jungle growth next to the estate.

"And there's a chance," said George, "he's in trouble and might not even be where we left him."

"We'll have to return to town and rent a boat," Nancy concluded.

The trio walked as fast as they could and made their way to the main highway. Bess pointed out that public transportation was infrequent along this route.

"Last time I was here I thought the bus would never come," she said.

The girls waited impatiently for twenty minutes. They were almost in despair when Nancy saw a familiar car headed in their direction.

"It's Lieutenant Masters!" she cried, holding up her hand to signal the officer.

The young woman stopped. "Hop in," she invited, and Nancy introduced her friends.

"Did you go to Heath Castle?" the officer asked.

"Yes," Nancy said. "We found several good leads. In fact, we were following one this morning. Salty came with us."

"Salty?"

"He's the singing clam digger of Muskoka River," Bess explained. "We left him on the beach. He may be in the hands of the thieves by now!"

Quickly Nancy explained the situation and asked the officer if she could arrange to send out a police boat to rescue Salty. "I'd like to go along if they'll let me," Nancy added. "I'm worried and feel responsible for him."

"We'll go too, if we may," put in George.

Lieutenant Masters radioed headquarters. In a few minutes she had arranged for the girls to accompany the rescue party. "But be careful," she warned them. "Meanwhile, I'll tell the chief to search for Biggs and Cobb."

On their way to the police dock, Lieutenant Masters said that she had planned to stop at the Drew home to discuss the problem of Joan Fenimore and Teddy Hooper.

"I had hoped Joan wouldn't play with Teddy any more," said Nancy.

"I'm inclined to think she may have tried not to," the officer said slowly, "but—well, here's the story. Teddy really causes me more worry than a dozen other boys on my list. He hasn't been to school for three days. It does no good to talk to his mother. She always sides with Teddy. I'm convinced she's unsuited to look after him."

"I'll say she is," George burst out, and told Lieutenant Masters about her stolen clothes. "We're sure he took them," she concluded.

Nancy said, "He's friendly with Biggs and Cobb." She explained about Teddy and the two men at the castle.

The lieutenant listened seriously. "I'm afraid the boy may be a thief," she agreed. "This morning I caught him trying to sell a pearl at Weatherby's curio shop. When I asked him where he had gotten it, he refused to answer me. Maybe he was the one who snatched your purse, Nancy. Anyway, when I took him home, his mother said she knew nothing about the pearl. Teddy finally said that Joan Fenimore had given it to him, but she denied this."

"What a pity he's involved her," Nancy said. "She's too nice a child."

A few minutes later Lieutenant Masters pulled up to the dock, where two officers were waiting in a motorboat.

The girls were introduced to Lieutenant Carney, a stocky, muscular-looking man, and Officer Mellon, who was tall and soft spoken.

The girls climbed aboard and the craft roared off. In a short time they reached the Heath estate. The rented motorboat was anchored in the same spot but there was no sign of Salty and his rowboat!

"He wouldn't have had time to row home," Bess said, worried. "And we didn't pass him on the way."

Lieutenant Carney cast anchor and everyone waded ashore. They started an intensive hunt. Before long George spotted the sailor lying motionless near the entrance to the cloister. She gasped. But suddenly he sat up and looked at her. "Thought ye'd never come," he muttered. There was blood on his face and shirt.

"Salty!" exclaimed Nancy, who had hurried over. "You're hurt!"

Her cry brought Lieutenant Carney on the run. Salty stood up and insisted he was all right, though he was somewhat unsteady.

"What happened?" Nancy asked, and Lieutenant Carney pulled out his notebook.

"I was diggin' for clams when a couple o'men an' a boy seemed to come right out o' nowhere. They asked me who I'd brought to the Heath gardens."

"Did you tell them?" Bess asked.

"No, but they said they'd beat me up if I didn't an' then go after the intruders themselves."

"I tried to argue 'em out o' it, but they was stubborn as mules. When they started to go after you, I tried to stop 'em."

"But there were three against you!" George said.

"Ye're right. 'Fraid I got knocked out. But I come to pretty soon; in fact, just in time to see one o' the rascals takin' my boat."

Salty told how he had seen one man going through the section of wall with the stone steps beyond and decided to follow. But the sailor had gone no farther than the opening before everything went black again before his eyes.

"Later I come to," he said, "but I couldn't seem to move for a while. Somewhere in the garden I heard two men talkin'. Nancy, you must be very careful from now on," he warned. "Those guys are plannin' to kidnap you!"

Lieutenant Carney spoke up. "We'd better get back to headquarters, Salty. You can give us a description of the men there. Also I want you to see a doctor to make sure you're all right."

In a few minutes the police boat was skimming down the river with Salty aboard. Nancy and her friends took the rented craft back to Campbell's Landing, then headed home in her car.

It was midafternoon when Nancy reached her house. She found Mr. Drew there, looking through some old newspapers. He and Nancy ate a late lunch while she eagerly showed him the photographs and the diary from the Heath estate.

"You certainly had an exciting time," her father remarked. "But I have some interesting news, too."

Nancy's eyes lighted with curiosity. "Something that will help solve the mystery, Dad?"

Her father nodded. "It concerns Juliana's missing nurse."

"Emily Foster?"

"Yes. I've located her. And here's the best part. Tomorrow morning she'll see you and tell you all she knows!"

CHAPTER XVI

News of Juliana

"OH, Dad! Where *is* Emily Foster?" Nancy asked, thrilled by the news. "How did you find her? What did she say about Juliana?"

"One question at a time, please," Mr. Drew said, laughing. "I talked to her only by telephone, so I didn't get any details."

"Is she here in River Heights?"

"No. In Hampton. I traced her by contacting the State Board of Nursing. Miss Foster is on a case in Hampton. She'll be free tomorrow, and has promised to meet us at the Hampton Motel."

"That's great. Maybe now we'll find Juliana!"

"Don't build your hopes too high," the lawyer warned his daughter. "Miss Foster may not know what became of the dancer. Even if she's able to provide a clue, you have only a short time to follow it up."

"That's the trouble," Nancy agreed, worried.

"Only ten days are left before Heath Castle will be lost to Juliana."

"Anyway, it seems to me you've built up a case against Daniel Hector, and that's something," her father said. "Even if Juliana is never found, there's no reason why that unscrupulous lawyer and his henchmen should help themselves to any of the estate."

The Drews planned to leave for Hampton that evening and spend the night at the motel in order to be on time for their early-morning appointment. Nancy, knowing she had a dozen things to do before leaving, rushed to do them.

Before they left, she suggested that they stop at the Fenimores' to see if Joan and her mother needed anything.

"I can't help worrying about them," she said.

Mr. Drew agreed. When they arrived at the house, the little girl was asleep. Her mother, however, was up and in surprisingly good spirits.

"The Hoopers have moved!" she said. "Now Joan and Teddy will be separated!"

"I wonder why they left so suddenly," Nancy mused.

"It was strange," Mrs. Fenimore replied. "Mrs. Hooper never talked about moving. A truck drove up with Mr. Hooper and another man and they loaded up all the furniture. Then Mrs. Hooper and Teddy left in a taxi with their luggage."

Mrs. Fenimore went on to say that Teddy had been boasting to Joan lately.

"He said his father was a smart man—he knew how to make money without working for it. Oh, how the talk frightened me!"

"I've never seen Mr. Hooper," Nancy said. "Can you describe him?"

"Cobb Hooper is a tall, thin man, sullen-faced, and unkempt in appearance."

"Did you say Cobb?" Nancy was startled by the name.

"Yes."

Nancy did not show her excitement as she recognized the name of the suspicious man she had overheard in the cloister at Heath Castle! She asked Mrs. Fenimore if she knew anything about Teddy and his family.

"I never knew when that boy was telling the truth," the woman replied. "But he told Joan he knew where there was a hidden treasure."

Nancy's mind was whirling as pieces of evidence seemed to fall into place. "Mrs. Fenimore," she asked, "did Joan ever talk to the Hoopers about Juliana and the property she was to inherit?"

"Dear me, yes! The child told everybody."

"And Teddy repeated it to his parents?"

"I don't know. He told Joan he went to the castle himself. But she was to keep it a secret."

"When did Teddy tell your daughter this?"

"Oh, some time ago."

There was nothing more of importance that Mrs. Fenimore could remember. After learning that the family was not in need of food or anything else, Nancy and her father got up to leave. Nancy remarked that they were on their way to interview a woman who might have information about Juliana.

"Oh, I hope she does!" Mrs. Fenimore said.

As soon as the Drews were in the car, Nancy told her father of her suspicion regarding Cobb Hooper.

"I thought Cobb was a last name," she commented. "It never occurred to me that Biggs' companion might be Teddy's father. The man I overheard in the cloister didn't act very paternally toward the boy."

"Maybe it's only a coincidence."

"Possibly. But Cobb is not a common name. Shouldn't we talk to the police again?"

Mr. Drew glanced at his watch. "All right. But we haven't much time if we're to get to Hampton tonight."

At headquarters the sergeant on duty consulted the files and informed the Drews that Cobb Hooper had a prison record.

"Have you a mug shot of him?" Carson Drew asked.

"Sure."

The photograph was brought out. With only

one glance Nancy knew that he was the same man she had seen in the castle garden.

"Cobb Hooper was one of the men who was hacking at the stone walls," she revealed. "He also rammed me with his boat."

"I'll try to get a warrant for his arrest," the officer said.

Nancy and her father thanked him and left for Hampton. They arrived at ten o'clock, and the next morning waited in the motel lobby to meet Emily Foster. She was fifteen minutes late.

"I'm sorry I couldn't make it on time," she said as she rushed in breathlessly. "You are Mr. and Miss Drew, aren't you?"

As the two nodded she went on, "The nurse who was to relieve me was late."

Nancy and her father liked Miss Foster at once. She was in her early forties, brisk and efficient, with a friendly smile.

After some polite conversation, she came right to the point. "Mr. Drew, you said over the telephone that you wanted to ask me about a former patient of mine. I'll be glad to help you if I can."

"The information we are seeking concerns Juliana Johnson," Mr. Drew began, "but I believe she gave the name Julia Flower at the hospital. She was injured in a hit-and-run accident." He showed Emily Foster Juliana's photograph.

"Yes, I knew her as Miss Flower," the nurse said.

"Tell us about her," Mr. Drew urged. "Whatever you can remember."

"Well, I had a hunch right away that Miss Flower gave us an assumed name," Emily Foster recalled. "For one thing, she never had any visitors. No messages came for her, no letters. She would not allow the authorities to notify anyone of her accident. 'I don't want anyone to know,' she would say. 'Not until I'm well.'"

"Did she believe she would recover?" Nancy asked quickly.

"Only in the beginning. Then the doctor told her the truth—that she'd be lame for the rest of her life."

"How did she take it?" Mr. Drew questioned.

"Very hard. Miss Flower cried for days, saying the strangest things. One remark I recall was, 'His little Cinderella will never dance for him again.' Oh, it was heartbreaking to listen to her."

Cinderella!

Nancy was so sure she was on the right track that her mind leaped from one possibility to another. She nearly missed hearing her father's next question.

"Where did Miss Flower go after she left the hospital?"

"I don't know," Miss Foster admitted regretfully. "From her remarks, I surmised she intended to live in some secluded place near Hopewell."

"That name Flower," Nancy mused. "Juliana was interested in gardening," she added, recalling what Mrs. Fenimore had told her about the dancer. "She would pick a place with flowers and trees and vegetables, probably a farm."

"Miss Flower no doubt did," the nurse said. "She was always asking me to buy her garden magazines. Why, the day before her release, I remember she cut an advertisement from the local paper—"

"What was it?" Nancy asked eagerly.

"The ad offered a small fruit and vegetable farm for sale—a place known as Clover Farm."

"Where is it?"

"It seems to me there used to be a Clover Farm at Milton about ten miles from here. I don't know whether it's the same one, though."

Nancy turned to her father.

He sensed her thoughts and said, "Yes, we'll go there today. It may be a futile trip, but we must follow every lead."

"Oh, I hope it's the right place!" said Nancy. "We must find Juliana soon. Time is getting short!"

CHAPTER XVII

Kidnapped!

AFTER the Drews had said good-by to Emily Foster, they drove toward Milton. At a service station near the edge of town, they stopped and inquired where Clover Farm was.

"Never heard of it," was the attendant's disappointing reply. He also did not know of a Julia Flower or Juliana or Julie Johnson. The local telephone book had no listing for any of the names.

"Oh, Dad," Nancy said, "have we run into another dead end?"

She had never felt more frustrated. Her father went into two shops to make the same inquiry, but had no better luck. A distressing thought came to Nancy that maybe the former dancer had moved to another part of the country or was no longer alive. Mr. Drew, trying to cheer his daughter, suggested that the elusive woman might be living in the area under another name.

At once Nancy took heart. "Let's drive all over this place. Maybe we'll pick up a clue."

Silence followed as they rode up one road and down another. About a mile out of town Nancy suddenly exclaimed, "Look!"

On one side of the road was an attractive white arched arbor at the entrance to the grounds. Fields of flowers, shrubs, and a nursery of trees lined either side. A neatly painted sign on the arbor read:

Jardin des Fleurs
Juliette Fleur, Prop.

"I'm sure this is the place!" Nancy cried excitedly. "Julia Flower translated her name into French, and calls her place Garden of Flowers."

It was a quarter of a mile to the house, which was surrounded by a high white picket fence with a locked gate. A terrier with a staccato bark raced from the building toward the callers.

"There's no bell or knocker," said Nancy. "How does one get in?"

Her question was answered when two gardeners hurried from the rear of the enclosure.

"No visitors allowed here!" one of them said curtly.

"We came to see Miss Fleur," Mr. Drew explained, then introduced himself and his daughter.

"Did she send for you?"

"No," Mr. Drew admitted, "but if she's the person we're looking for, we have important information for her."

Nancy pulled out Juliana's photograph, and showed it to the men, who stared at it. Finally one of them said, "It's her, all right—when she was younger. But she's not here!"

"Where is she?" Nancy asked.

"Well, usually she never leaves the place on account of being such a cripple. But when that government man came for her last night, she had to go. He took her away in a car."

"What government man?" Mr. Drew asked quickly. "Did he give his name?"

"He probably told Miss Fleur. We didn't hear it."

"Did she say why she had to go with him?" Nancy asked.

"It was something about income tax. Miss Fleur always thought she paid the government every penny she owed. She's very honest. But the man claimed she'd made a false report and might have to go to prison."

"This seems very irregular to me," Mr. Drew commented. "Even if Miss Fleur made a mistake in the amount of her tax, she would not be sentenced without a hearing. The usual procedure is to notify the accused by letter and have the person call at the tax office to explain his or her side of the matter."

"Dad," Nancy said, "it looks as if someone was very eager to get Miss Fleur away from here. We must find her!"

"First of all, we'll check with the Internal Revenue Service; that is, if I can use a telephone."

The two gardeners, sensing that Nancy and her father were sincere, invited them into the farmhouse. Mr. Drew called. When he finished, he looked grim.

"Just as we feared," he revealed. "The Internal Revenue Service has no case pending against Juliette Fleur, Juliana Johnson, or Julia Flower."

"Then it was a hoax!" Nancy exclaimed.

"Yes. The man who came here was an impostor."

The gardeners suddenly looked alarmed. One of them said, "Are you saying Miss Fleur maybe was kidnapped?"

"Possibly," Mr. Drew replied.

The two workmen were speechless. "Oh, find her!" one said. "We think an awful lot of her."

"Have you any idea where she may have been taken?" Nancy asked. Both men said they had told her everything they knew.

They spread the news of the incident to Miss Fleur's other two employees who came in from the fields. Their faces became sad.

"Those kidnappers may hurt her!" one of the gardeners said.

"I wouldn't worry about that," Mr. Drew said

to comfort the man. "Miss Fleur probably will receive good treatment. But unfortunately she will lose a fortune unless she can be found."

"But how? Shall we call the police?" the man asked.

"We'll stop at headquarters on the way home," Mr. Drew said, and promised the gardeners he would do everything he could to find Juliette Fleur.

"Tell me, what did the alleged government man look like?" he asked.

The gardeners' description was not very helpful.

"He was tall and slender," one said, "and wore dark glasses. He had a beard and a mustache."

"Probably a disguise," Nancy concluded.

After the Drews had told their story to the local police, they returned to the Hampton Motel. On their way to the dining room, Carson Drew purchased a copy of the River Heights newspaper. A startling headline caught his eyes:

FAMOUS DANCER RETURNS IN TIME TO CLAIM HEATH FORTUNE

The article stated that after a long search, Daniel Hector had found the missing Juliana, who now was staying at the Riverview Hotel in River Heights. For many years the famous dancer had been fulfilling professional engagements in South America under another name.

"So that's what Hector has been up to!" Nancy said hotly. "He had the real Juliana kidnapped to be able to present this impostor!"

"It certainly seems that way," Mr. Drew agreed.

"If Daniel Hector can establish the impostor as the heiress, he will probably pay her well and then take over the estate."

"Let's hurry back to River Heights," Nancy suggested.

After hastening through lunch she and her father checked out of the motel, and soon were driving along the road toward home.

"I wonder where the abductor has hidden Juliana," Nancy said.

It was early afternoon when the Drews reached River Heights. The lawyer said he had to stop in his office for a couple of hours and that Nancy could use the car in the meantime.

"I think I'll go see Mrs. Fenimore and find out whether she has heard the news," Nancy decided as she got out of the car. She drove off and turned in the direction of the little house.

Joan and her mother were happy to see her. They had not read the newspapers, however, and had not heard from Daniel Hector. When Nancy told them about the article, Mrs. Fenimore became excited.

"You mean my sister has really been found? Oh, I just can't believe it! Where is she?"

"Mrs. Fenimore," Nancy said, "I don't want to

disappoint you, but I believe that the woman Hector claims to have located is an impostor!"

"What do you mean?" Mrs. Fenimore looked bewildered.

Nancy told about the result of her investigation and of her suspicion that the real Juliana had been kidnapped.

"But that's terrible," Mrs. Fenimore finally said. "It's an unscrupulous scheme to cheat my sister out of her inheritance, and who knows, she might be a prisoner of Hector's for years! We must tell the police!"

"I wish we could," Nancy said. "But so far I can't prove anything. Unless we find your sister in time, Hector may get away with his crooked scheme."

"But I can tell if the claimant is my sister, can't I?"

"I don't know whether your word against hers would be proof enough. Anyway, I think we should meet the dancer who claims to be Juliana."

Joan insisted upon coming along, and soon the three of them arrived at the Riverview Hotel.

"You mean Señora Fernandez?" the desk clerk replied when Nancy inquired for the woman. "I'll see if she's receiving callers."

Mrs. Fenimore became more and more apprehensive as they waited. Finally the clerk told them to go up to Room 320. They knocked and a voice said, "Come in!"

A beautiful woman was reclining on the bed, her back braced by several embroidered pillows. She wore an exotic negligee which set off to advantage her dark hair and creamy white skin.

"Vera! I am so glad to see you again!" she said and got up to embrace Mrs. Fenimore. "And this is Joan, isn't it?" She kissed the little girl lightly on the cheek.

Mrs. Fenimore was so confused that for a moment she could not speak. Nancy broke the silence by giving her name.

"Miss Drew?" the dancer looked perplexed but only for an instant. "Yes, I believe Mr. Hector told me about you."

By now Mrs. Fenimore had relaxed. "Julie, why did you go away?"

"I—I eloped with my Mexican husband."

"But how could you desert Walter Heath?"

"I couldn't marry him, because I didn't love him. But I didn't want to hurt him either; that's why I disappeared."

"But now you've come back to claim his fortune," Nancy put in. "By the way, what are your plans for the estate?"

"I'll sell it. Mr. Hector has a buyer for it already."

"Then you won't stay in River Heights?" Mrs. Fenimore asked.

"Of course not. I have my career and my home in Mexico."

Mrs. Fenimore looked at the woman calmly. "Mr. Hector won't be able to sell the estate for you because you are not my sister!"

The other woman blanched. "I may have changed in those ten years, but I can prove who I am!"

"How?" Nancy asked quickly.

"I have all necessary identification. And I also have this!" From beneath her pillow the dancer brought out a torn paper. Nancy instantly knew that it was the missing half of the note she had found at the Heath factory. She read the words:

> day the sec-
> am hiding
> may make me
> Then I shall be
> of you. Love,
>   Walt

Nancy did not have the other half of the note with her, but she knew its contents by heart. The complete message would read:

> Dear C,
>   Someday the sec-
> cret which I am hiding
> in a wall may make me
> famous. Then I shall be
> worthy of you. Love,
>   Walt

The young sleuth concluded that Walter Heath had not sold the formula on which he had been working. Instead, he had hidden the dyes somewhere in the old estate walls to keep them safe from men like Biggs.

"Do you have the other half of the note?" Nancy asked Señora Fernandez.

"No, I lost it years ago."

"What does the C stand for?"

"Oh—Walt used to call me Carita. It was a nickname he gave me when we first met."

"You are not my sister!" Mrs. Fenimore cried out again. She could hardly control her anger. "And this note proves nothing!"

Nancy took her arm. "Let's go now. And don't worry," she said as the three left.

Back on the street, Nancy said, "Daniel Hector did a good job. Señora Fernandez does resemble your sister, doesn't she?"

Mrs. Fenimore nodded. "So much so that at first I wasn't sure myself."

"I noticed the woman had rather large feet," Nancy said. "She must wear at least a size nine or ten shoe."

"And Juliana had extremely small feet," Mrs. Fenimore remarked. "That should help prove Mrs. Fernandez is a phony."

"Yes. Please don't worry about it. Right now all I'm concerned about is finding your sister!"

Nancy dropped the Fenimores off at their house

"You are not my sister!" Mrs. Fenimore cried out.

and drove home. On the way she passed Bess's house and noticed that George's car stood in front.

"I'll stop to tell them the latest news about the case," Nancy decided.

Bess invited both girls to stay to dinner. Nancy accepted after calling Hannah Gruen.

"Your father won't be back until late, anyway," the housekeeper said.

By the time Nancy arrived home, it was dark. As she pulled into the driveway, the young detective noticed that there were no lights on in the house.

"That's funny," she thought, stopping. "Whenever Hannah goes out, she leaves a lamp on."

Nancy hurried to the front door. With a surge of alarm she found it standing slightly ajar. Cautiously she pushed it open but saw only the dark hallway.

"Hannah!" she called out, reaching for the hall switch.

Before she could turn on the lights, a powerful arm seized her and a hand was clapped over her mouth. At the same time the assailant yanked her into the hall and slammed the door shut!

CHAPTER XVIII

Tower Trouble

THE man held Nancy in an iron grip, and though she struggled, she could not break away. Did she know him? He kept in back of her, so she could not see his face.

Frightening questions raced through her mind: *Where was Hannah? Had the housekeeper been harmed?*

"We're going to take you for a little ride now," her captor said in a whisper. "You're through meddling at Heath Castle!"

"Will you shut up!" a harsh voice put in. The second man tied a scarf over her eyes. "Let's get her out of here before her father comes home."

Suddenly Nancy had an idea of how to throw the men off guard. With a moan she slumped into her captor's arms and dropped her purse.

He exclaimed angrily, "She's fainted!"

"So what?" snapped the other. "We follow the

orders. I'll get the car and bring it up the driveway. You carry her out when I signal."

Her body limp, but her senses sharply alert, Nancy waited for her chance to escape. When the other man left, her captor released his grasp. Instead of crumpling to the floor, Nancy pulled off the scarf and dashed up the stairs to her father's room.

The man gave a startled cry and ran after her. But Nancy locked the door before he reached it.

"I'm calling the police!" she shouted, and raced to the telephone.

For a few moments the intruder pounded on the door wildly, and banged himself against it, then suddenly stopped. Nancy had just finished dialing when she heard him run downstairs and slam the front door.

Quickly she reported the incident to headquarters, then went to look out the window. She saw the intruder round the end of the drive and flee into the darkness. Despite the thumping of her heart, she smiled grimly.

As Nancy hurried through the house she switched on the lights and called Hannah's name. She found the housekeeper gagged and tied to a chair in the kitchen.

"Are you all right?" Nancy asked anxiously as she released the woman.

"I'm not hurt," Hannah said hoarsely. "But the nerve of those two!" She added angrily, "I was expecting you or your father, and when the bell rang I thought one of you had forgotten your key. I didn't look out, just opened the door. Those men pushed right in, turned off the lights, and tied me up in my own kitchen!"

A few minutes later two officers arrived. Hannah described one intruder as tall and thin, the other as short, stocky, and powerfully built. Both were masked. Nancy suspected they were Cobb and Biggs.

"They must have been watching for me," she said, "because they apparently knew my father was out. Also, they were careful to park some distance away, so I wouldn't see a strange car in front of the house."

Before leaving, one of the policemen called headquarters and arranged for a plainclothesman to keep an eye on the Drew house that night in case the suspects made another attempt to kidnap Nancy.

Mr. Drew arrived home half an hour later. He listened, deeply concerned, as his daughter and the housekeeper told what had happened.

"You're a brave and clever girl," he said to Nancy, "but from now on you must be extra careful. Obviously these men are desperate to get you off this case."

"Someone is giving them orders," she said. "I have a hunch it's Daniel Hector."

That night Nancy lay awake long after the

others in the house were asleep. "The kidnappers wanted to keep me from going to Heath Castle," she reasoned. "Surely not because of anything I've seen there already. It must be because of something else hidden in the place."

An amazing idea struck her. Nancy could hardly wait to call Bess and George. Early the next morning she phoned them.

"What time is it?" Bess asked sleepily. Finally she became awake enough to say yes to Nancy's request that the three girls go out to the Heath estate.

"Okay," Bess said, "but let's play it safe. I don't want to be scared to death again."

George was eager for the adventure. She put a flashlight and police whistle into her pants pocket. All three girls left notes at their homes since the families were not yet up. Nancy added to hers, "Please phone Lieutenant Masters where I am. I want to follow up a hunch connected with the mystery out there."

When Nancy picked up the cousins in her car, they demanded a full explanation of the day's mission.

"It's my opinion that Daniel Hector or one of his men kidnapped the real Juliana," Nancy said. "He'll hold her until Señora Fernandez can establish her claim to the fortune. He'll take the lion's share of it and then disappear."

"But what does Heath Castle have to do with

it?" Bess asked. "Do you think Juliana is imprisoned there?"

"Yes, I do. Mr. Hector found out recently that I was hot on the trail of the real Juliana and he had to get her out of the way. What better hiding place for his prisoner than the castle? Then, of course, he'd have to keep me away from there, so he tried to have me kidnapped."

"Your reasoning sounds logical," George admitted. "The crippled woman could have been brought to the place the night she left Jardin des Fleurs."

At the estate Nancy and her friends scaled the wall and dropped to the ground. As the three made their way toward the castle, they did not see nor hear the dogs.

"What worries me," said Nancy, "is whether we can get in. Of course, I have a key to the front door, but it may have been padlocked."

When they reached it the girls were amazed to find the door ajar.

"Hector may be here," Bess whispered worriedly. "Or perhaps Cobb and Biggs."

There was not a sound of anyone stirring about the premises. Noiselessly, Nancy and the girls slipped inside the castle.

"I have a hunch," Nancy whispered, "that Juliana is imprisoned in the tower, not in this building. Let's look there first."

The girls tiptoed along the winding corridor to

the courtyard garden where the entrances to the towers were. Nancy tried the door of the one in which she had been imprisoned. It was unlocked.

"Will you two please stand guard while I go upstairs?" she asked her friends.

They nodded, and Nancy ascended the circular iron staircase. She was gone several minutes. Bess was becoming uneasy about her friend when she heard Nancy returning.

"No one there," the young detective reported. "I looked out over the grounds, too, but didn't see anything suspicious."

"Where next?" George asked.

"Here's a trap door," Nancy replied, pointing toward the floor. "What it opens into I haven't been able to find out. But some tools that weren't here before are in that corner now. I believe someone left them to lift the trap door."

Carefully Nancy inserted a finely edged tool in the crack, then slipped a thin chisel through the space and depressed a catch. Using a crowbar, the girls raised the heavy metal door.

Cautiously they peered into the darkness below. Nancy and George snapped on their flashlights. They revealed a flight of iron steps leading into a long corridor. Grilled doors opened from it.

"Anyone down there?" Nancy called.

No answer. Her own voice echoed weirdly. Just then Nancy thought she heard a sound like a moan. She hurried down the stairway, followed by Bess and George. Several cells lined one wall.

Nancy flashed her light into the first cell. It was a tiny room, musty and dark. The only visible sunlight filtered in through a high, barred window.

"These rooms look like old dungeons," Bess commented with a little shiver.

"Probably the Heaths used them for storing food and other things," George said.

The next two cells were empty. But as the girls approached the fourth, they distinctly heard someone moan. Pausing to listen, they caught a pitiful cry from the far end of the corridor.

"Let me out! Let me out! Please help me!"

Nancy, Bess, and George hurried up the passageway. A small woman, crippled and weak, had pulled herself to the grilled doorway. She clung there, frightened and beseeching.

"Juliana Johnson!" Nancy said, recognizing the lovely face in Mrs. Fenimore's photographs.

"No! No!" The prisoner shrank back. "I am Miss Fleur."

"We'll talk about that later," Nancy told her kindly, and unbolted the door.

She and Bess assisted the woman along the musty corridor, while George beamed the flashlights. It was slow work because of Juliana's weak condition.

Nancy introduced herself and the girls. "We've

come to help you," she added. "Who brought you here?"

"Have you been mistreated?" Bess put in.

"I've had enough to eat and drink," the former dancer said. "But I've been so perplexed."

Questioned by Nancy, she revealed what had happened to her. A man, who had shown an identification card of a government agent, had taken her away from Jardin des Fleurs in a car.

"It was dark when we reached this place. I was hurried inside and locked in the cell. I was told it was because of not paying enough income tax," she ended the story. "What does it all mean?"

"That's not true," Nancy replied. "My father inquired. A great deal has happened since you left your home ten years ago," she added.

"I—I don't know what you're talking about!"

"You are Juliana Johnson," Nancy said with quiet conviction. "Why not admit it?"

"No, no, never!"

"Do you realize where you are now?" Nancy asked, taking a different tack. "You are at Heath Castle."

"Heath Castle! You mean—Walt—?"

"Walter Heath died a number of years ago," Nancy said gently. "He loved you to the end and willed all his property to you."

"Walt—dead!" the woman whispered. "Then he thought of me as I used to be—beautiful, and a talented dancer."

"He loved you for yourself," Bess spoke up. "Not for your fame."

Juliana brushed a wisp of straggling gray hair from her eyes. Her slumping shoulders stiffened.

"But I've lost all my beauty!" she cried out. "Oh, I want to be left alone. I have my farm. Take me back there, please!"

"You mean you don't want Heath Castle?" George asked.

"I loved Heath Castle, and I loved Walt," Juliana said brokenly. "But I hid myself away so that he never would see me in this condition. Perhaps this is foolish pride, but it seems best that I finish out my days as I am doing."

"Your sister Vera wants to be with you very much," said Nancy. "She is a widow now with a little girl who looks a great deal like you."

Juliana was deeply moved. "Vera has a daughter?" she murmured. "Where is she?"

"The child's name is Joan. She and her mother, now Mrs. Fenimore, live in River Heights. Joan likes flowers and gardening, just as you do. I can't tell you the whole story now, but the two of them need you."

"If I had known before—" Juliana began. "At the beginning of my retirement I sent a letter to my sister but it came back. I had no idea where she was."

"Mrs. Fenimore and Joan want to leave the neighborhood where they live," Nancy put in.

"Joan would be so happy in these surroundings."

"Are the gardens still beautiful?" the former dancer asked dreamily.

Nancy hated to tell the woman the truth. She tried to soften it by saying, "They have been badly neglected. But they could be landscaped again. However, only a person who truly loved the place would want to do it."

"To me it would be a challenge," Juliana said with sudden spirit. "A memorial to Walt. But the castle and its grounds really are pretty large for three people."

"What a wonderful place it would be for handicapped children!" Bess mused.

"And I'd like to help them!" Juliana announced. "Yes, I'll make this place a beautiful spot again! I'll bring Joan and Vera here. And later we'll see about the other children."

"Good!" Nancy said. "We'll take you right to your sister, and then I'll go to settle my score with Mr. Hector."

The group had finally reached the foot of the stairway. Before the former dancer could be helped up the steps, a sardonic laugh echoed down to them.

"I'll make sure you don't get out!" a voice threatened.

The next instant the trap door dropped into place with a crash. A heavy object was placed on top of it. Then all was quiet in the dungeon!

CHAPTER XIX

Release and Capture

NANCY darted up the stairway to try opening the trap door. As she had feared, it did not budge. George and Bess pushed with all their might.

"It's hopeless," said Bess, panting.

"We're all prisoners!" Juliana Johnson exclaimed.

Nancy was fearful this new shock might undermine Juliana's health completely, so she said, "I feel sure there's no cause for alarm. When we fail to show up, help will come. I left a note at home."

"But will the trap door be noticed by anyone?" Juliana asked dubiously.

"Perhaps I can find another exit," Nancy said.

While Bess remained with Juliana, Nancy and George, using flashlights, searched the various cells. They could find no exit. The only openings were the high grilled windows.

"Nancy," George said suddenly, "I brought a police whistle. Suppose I blow it."

"Great!" said Nancy. "If you stand on my shoulders, you should be able to reach one of the windows and signal for help."

George and Nancy stepped into the nearest cell and went to the window. With agility George climbed to Nancy's shoulders and clung to the iron grills of the window. She blew a dozen shrill blasts with her whistle.

"I hope it'll work," she said, after dropping lightly to the floor.

She and Nancy wondered how long they might have to wait and how long Juliana could stand the added strain. They returned to the others and sat down on the steps.

Juliana had lapsed into silence, but Nancy gradually drew her out. One of the first questions Nancy asked was whether or not Walter Heath had given her a large pearl.

"No, but he was going to. It was being made into a ring when I went away."

Nancy next inquired if Juliana's fiancé had had a special name for her.

"Yes. He called me his little Cinderella," she said, smiling at the recollection. "Once Walt asked me to put on one of my dancing slippers and make a print in a block of newly made cement. He said he was going to set it in the garden wall opposite Poet's Nook. I suppose it was a lover's foolish idea."

"That wasn't foolish," Nancy replied. "It was very sensible. That footprint clue in the crumbling wall will prove your right to the Heath fortune against any claim of an impostor!"

Juliana said, "Please tell me the whole story. I am terribly confused." As kindly as she could, Nancy related all she knew.

"How dreadful!" Juliana exclaimed. "And what harrowing experiences you have had!"

"Tell me something," said Nancy. "It was reported that the hospital found a lot of money on you. Did you plan to stay away a long time?"

"Oh no. I was going to buy an expensive personal gift for Walt from a man who wanted cash. Also I planned to purchase something for our home." The former dancer sighed deeply.

Suddenly the woman slumped forward. In an instant Nancy caught her and placed the limp body on the floor.

"Juliana has fainted!" Bess cried out.

Nancy was fearful that the woman was suffering from something more serious than a faint, because the former dancer's pulse was very weak. Under the flashlight her face looked chalk-white.

"The poor woman!" Bess murmured. "She has been through so much!"

The girls tried to revive Juliana, and finally succeeded.

"We *must* get out of here!" said Nancy.

At that moment they heard distant shouts outside.

"Listen!" George commanded.

The voices were coming closer. George blew several loud blasts on her whistle.

"Where are you?" somebody called. "We're the police. There are four of us."

Nancy shouted that they were below the trap door in the tower. She called out directions and in another five minutes the four prisoners were released.

"Lieutenant Masters!" exclaimed Nancy. "How glad I am to see you! Did my father get in touch with you?"

"No. Hannah Gruen did. And who is this?" she asked, smiling at the former dancer.

Juliana herself replied to the question. When Nancy suggested that she ought not to expend her strength talking, the woman insisted she felt much better.

"Who shut you in here?" the policewoman demanded.

"I'm not sure," Nancy answered. "The voice was disguised, I think. But it might have been Daniel Hector. He must have escaped."

"Oh, no, he didn't," said a voice triumphantly. "We nabbed him climbing over a wall. Also these two birds."

Two more policemen appeared. With them,

handcuffed, were Cobb and Biggs. Behind the men was Daniel Hector.

"This is an outrage!" the lawyer snapped. "You can't arrest me. I have a perfect right to be on this property. The others are trespassing."

Coolly Nancy presented her evidence against the lawyer. She accused him of stealing jewelry from the estate, a claim that could be proved by photographs found in Walter Heath's box.

"And that's not the worst," she said to him. "You pretended to look for the woman who was to inherit the estate. But when you did locate her you kept it a secret so you could help yourself to the estate. When you found out I was on the trail of the real Juliana Johnson, you had her kidnapped and locked in the dungeon here! To protect yourself, you produced an impostor with whom you had made a bargain."

"Ridiculous!" Hector cried furiously. "Lies—lies! Nothing but lies!"

Hector had not seen Juliana yet. She was seated on the winding stairs in the tower behind Nancy. The young sleuth now stepped aside. Hector stared at the crippled dancer.

"So what?" he demanded after a moment. "I had nothing to do with bringing her here! And she can't prove she's the missing dancer. Just look at her!"

"Oh, yes, I can prove it," Juliana retorted with

spirit. "The imprint of my dancing shoe is embedded in a wall at Heath Castle. Furthermore, I still have the slipper that made the imprint!"

"What's that got to do with it? The real Juliana is at the Riverview Hotel!" the lawyer blustered. "She has a note to prove her identity. A note signed Walt."

"Don't you mean half a note?" Nancy asked. "I have the rest!"

Cobb and Biggs looked startled. "You?" Biggs cried. "Where did you find it?"

"At the factory after the explosion."

The three men hung their heads guiltily, admitting they had been there. Biggs added, "Hooper here found the note in a desk Hector sold. He tore it in two pieces, expecting the lawyer to put up more money for the second half. When one piece was lost, we thought Hector had found it."

In answer to Nancy's question if he were Teddy's father, the man nodded sullenly.

Nancy explained to Juliana that Teddy had learned about the estate from Joan. Teddy had told his father that Juliana was missing. Cobb and Biggs got together. Biggs suspected his former employer had hidden some valuable things in the estate walls and the two men convinced Hector he ought to hire them to look for the treasure. When they found a few items, the men kept them.

"You guessed right, but I can't figure out how," said Biggs.

"I know nothing about all this!" shouted the lawyer.

"Yes, you do," Cobb Hooper said bitterly. "You were behind the whole thing. You brought the dogs to guard the estate, but later I kept 'em tied up and then took 'em back to the kennel."

"We were afraid of them ourselves," Biggs added.

"Mr. Hector," said Lieutenant Masters, "it looks as if the case against you is pretty serious."

"I tell you I never saw these men before," the lawyer insisted. "Nor that crippled woman, either. Now all of you get out of here!"

For a long second there was silence. Then Juliana slowly got to her feet. Her eyes ablaze, she pointed a finger at Hector and exclaimed:

"Arrest that man! Arrest him for kidnapping!"

The wily lawyer's jaw dropped. Then he recovered. "The woman is crazy!" he shouted.

"The night you came to my farm and brought me here you wore a disguise," Juliana said accusingly. "At first I didn't recognize you. But your voice—I know your voice." Her eyes snapped with anger as she added, "I will bring charges against you to the fullest extent of the law for Walter Heath's sake!"

Daniel Hector knew he was beaten. But he

would not give up yet. He glared at Nancy and cried out:

"If you had minded your own business, there wouldn't have been all this trouble! But don't be so smug. You think there are treasures and money for Juliana. You're wrong. There's nothing in the estate but debts. She has inherited a wreck!"

CHAPTER XX

A Last Surprise

"NOTHING in the estate!" Nancy exclaimed. "What do you mean?"

The angry lawyer refused to reply. He and the other prisoners were led away by the police. Nancy, Miss Masters, and Juliana headed for the Fenimore home. When they arrived, Juliana asked Nancy to go in first and break the news.

"Oh, you've found my sister!" Mrs. Fenimore cried, after Nancy had told her. "You wonderful girl! I don't care if we never have Heath Castle. To think Juliana is alive, and we can be together again!"

Gently Nancy warned her about Juliana's condition. The news was a shock, but Mrs. Fenimore took it bravely as Juliana was brought in. The sisters embraced and both cried a little. Then over and over the joyful women expressed their gratitude to Nancy.

The young sleuth said she was glad to have accomplished what she had, but was not satisfied to leave the case yet. For days afterward she was tormented by all the distressing angles of the affair.

In the meantime, Juliana had claimed her inheritance and had requested that all legal matters be attended to by Mr. Drew. The lawyer had lost no time in having Hector and the other men prosecuted, and also brought charges against the woman who had impersonated the dancer.

"Hooper and Biggs admit having found several bottles of dye and a formula marked, 'Perfected Formula,' hidden in the cloister walls," Mr. Drew told Nancy. "They've surrendered them and I've had an analysis made. The dye has dried up but a newly made liquid would be of great value commercially if produced under the same conditions that Walter Heath used."

"What were they?" Nancy asked.

"Sea salt was mixed with the spring water in the pond. Marine whelks, which are a huge type of mollusk, were imported and put into it. They exude a beautiful purple dye. After Heath's death the whelks vanished."

Nancy was thoughtful. "It would take a good bit of money to start up that business, wouldn't it?"

"Yes," her father replied. "But it would be

profitable for Juliana. The special shade of purple is difficult to imitate synthetically."

Nancy had been hoping that Hector's dire statement regarding the estate would not be true, but part of it was. Mr. Drew had learned that the total Heath assets were twenty dollars, the walled grounds, and a ruined castle with a few pieces of furniture. The debts, however, were illegal loans, which Hector had made against the estate and which he would have to pay back.

Account books had been falsified to show that huge sums had been paid to various detective agencies, supposedly for the purpose of conducting a search for the missing Juliana. But the wily lawyer had kept the money.

"Unfortunately we can't recover it," Mr. Drew remarked to his daughter. "Hector has spent it all and has little of his own left."

"How about the Heath pearl, Dad? You didn't find it?"

"No. I'll keep on trying, of course. Frankly, I don't feel hopeful."

"Somewhere on those grounds," said Nancy, "there must be something of value hidden. After all, Walter Heath told Sam Weatherby there was another treasure."

"I've had the place searched, Nancy. Workmen even removed the imprinted block of cement below the wall fountain, but there was nothing behind it. Heath Castle will have to be sold.

"But I'm afraid," he went on, "the sale price won't be much, considering its present condition. Juliana wants to keep the property, but she can't. She has barely enough funds to operate Jardin des Fleurs."

It was some consolation to Nancy that she had brought the sisters together, but she felt as if she had failed in one of the most vital tasks of her life.

"Even if I did find Juliana, I wasn't able to save the estate or help the Fenimores financially. And they need money so badly."

Unwilling to give up, Nancy drove out to the estate one day after lunch to try to find the treasure which Walter Heath had mentioned.

"What can it be and where?" she asked herself. "It's supposed to be in plain sight."

Nancy worked her way doggedly through the neglected grounds and examined the statuary. Though not an expert, she could tell that none of it was unusual. She looked at a grove of fruit trees which might become a source of profit. But the trees were too old.

Finally the young detective, hot, thirsty, and discouraged, arrived at the little garden off the cloister. As Nancy walked toward the fountain, she suddenly stopped short and stared at the sparkling stream of water.

"That's it!" she exclaimed softly. "Spring water! Cold, clear, delicious, and probably pure. It might even have minerals in it!"

Nancy could visualize the estate as a health resort where people came to rest and drink the water.

"Or it could be bottled and sold!" she thought.

Excited by the idea, Nancy quenched her thirst, then hurried home to telephone her father. He promised to have the spring tested in the morning.

The next afternoon the Drews were delighted to learn that the water was pure and rich in minerals. A further search of the grounds revealed several more beneficial springs.

"The supply is plentiful," Nancy told Bess and George. "Dad will probably make arrangements with a bottling company to market it."

In the meantime Nancy had remembered the beautiful shells she had found in the pond. Saying nothing to Juliana, she sent one of them to a company in New York which specialized in making fine mother-of-pearl jewelry. The answer came back promptly: the firm would buy at a good price all similar shells.

"Nancy, you're wonderful!" exclaimed Juliana when Nancy telephoned her about it.

The bottling company also offered financial backing to convert part of the castle and grounds into a health resort.

"That's wonderful!" Juliana cried out. "Now I can afford to turn a section of the castle and grounds into a free vacation spot for handicapped children, and, of course, my sister and Joan and I will occupy some of the rooms.

"You've certainly changed our lives, Nancy," she added gratefully. "And now the Heath property will become beautiful again!"

A year later, upon invitation, Nancy, Bess, George, Mr. Drew, and Lieutenant Masters journeyed to the estate to view the many changes. The great gate stood open. The visitors drove up a winding road between avenues of trimmed hedge and trees. The three girls smiled when they recalled how different everything had seemed to them on their former trips there.

"It doesn't make me feel a bit creepy now," Bess remarked.

"Those penetrating eyes that spied on us from behind the evergreen," Nancy said, "were Hooper's or Biggs'."

"With Cobb Hooper in jail, what has become of Mrs. Hooper and Teddy?" asked George.

"She's working," the policewoman replied. "Teddy has been sent to a special school, where he's doing very well."

The visitors got out of the car near the restored loggia and paused to admire the repairs to the crumbling walls. The gardens were a mass of bloom. The lawn in front of the castle was velvety smooth with no weeds.

"How did Juliana ever accomplish so much in such a short time?" George asked.

Nancy replied, "She imported her gardeners from Jardin des Fleurs."

Bess called the girls' attention to the children who had come out on the lawn to play. A few were in wheelchairs, but they pushed themselves about with amazing skill.

"Juliana is doing remarkable work with these youngsters," said Lieutenant Masters. "She's putting new spirit into them. Joan is developing into a fine little girl, too. She's proving to be a great help to her aunt."

"What is she doing?" Bess asked.

"Juliana, with the help of a therapist, teaches exercises to the children to restore nimbleness to their bodies. Joan does the demonstrating. And incidentally, Joan is the delight of her aunt. She's going to be a wonderful dancer someday."

"And carry on from where Juliana left off," Bess said dreamily.

The callers were greeted cordially by the mistress of Heath Castle and her sister, Mrs. Fenimore, now restored to health and looking very attractive with a fashionable new hairdo. Both women thanked Bess and George for their excellent assistance to Nancy in solving the mystery.

Joan hugged Nancy and the others happily. "Oh, come see my garden," she exclaimed, and showed them a small plot of beautifully tended flowers in front of the castle.

Tea was served on the terrace. Afterward, Juliana led her guests to the little garden where Nancy had discovered the spring. Children were playing on the shady walks.

"The water is helping to build strong bodies," Juliana said proudly. "Oh, it means so much to me to bring these boys and girls here! I'd never have forgiven myself if I had returned to a lonely life at Jardin des Fleurs. By the way, I sold it at a nice profit."

Mr. Drew had been waiting for this very moment. He took a tiny box from his pocket and slipped it into Juliana's hand.

"A little surprise," he explained, smiling.

The woman slowly raised the lid. Nestled in purple velvet was a ring set with a huge pearl.

"Not the one Walt meant for me?" Juliana asked, dazed.

"Yes."

"But how did you recover it? I thought Mr. Hector had found the ring and sold it."

"He had, but Dad was able to trace it," Nancy spoke up. "Mr. Hector failed to notice the inscription inside."

Tears filled Juliana's eyes as she read, " 'To my Cinderella.' I'll wear the ring always in memory of Walt," she whispered, her voice trembling. "Oh, Nancy, my dear friend—and Mr. Drew, and Bess and George, and Lieutenant Masters, also my dear friends—you've made me very, very happy."

The young detective smiled, glad that everything had worked out so successfully. Her gaze wandered along the stately cloister of Heath Castle. With the afternoon sun sinking low, the shadowy passageway had never looked more beautiful.

It was peaceful and quiet, and nothing was further from Nancy's thoughts than a new mystery. Yet in a short time she would be working on another exciting case called, *Mystery of the Tolling Bell.*

"Don't thank me for helping you, Juliana," she said earnestly, taking the woman's hand. "Thank the crumbling walls. They contained the clues that brought you here. To me Heath Castle will always remain a symbol of mystery and romance."

Match Wits with The Hardy Boys®!

Collect the Complete
Hardy Boys Mystery Stories®
by Franklin W. Dixon

The Hardy Boys Back-to-Back

Celebrate over 70 Years with the World's Greatest Super Sleuths!

Match Wits with Super Sleuth Nancy Drew!

Collect the Complete
Nancy Drew Mystery Stories®
by Carolyn Keene

Celebrate over 70 years with the World's Best Detective